Living with Yourself

About the Author

Hanni Lane grew up in a small town in the English countryside, before moving to London to study fashion design. An author of young adult and teen fiction, her debut novel Living with Yourself was written through personal challenges, where writing can often feel like a respite from the day. She is dedicated to writing about less-spoken topics; ones she has struggled with or believes could help others. When Hanni is not writing, she is designing and making sustainable clothes, advocating for garment workers' rights, singing too loud, dancing and spending time with family.

Hanni Lane

Living with Yourself

Olympia Publishers
London

www.olympiapublishers.com
OLYMPIA PAPERBACK EDITION

Copyright © Hanni Lane 2024

The right of Hanni Lane to be identified as author of
this work has been asserted in accordance with sections 77 and 78 of
the Copyright, Designs and Patents Act 1988.

All Rights Reserved

No reproduction, copy or transmission of this publication
may be made without written permission.
No paragraph of this publication may be reproduced,
copied or transmitted save with the written permission of the publisher,
or in accordance with the provisions
of the Copyright Act 1956 (as amended).

Any person who commits any unauthorised act in relation to
this publication may be liable to criminal
prosecution and civil claims for damage.

A CIP catalogue record for this title is
available from the British Library.

ISBN: 978-1-80074-639-8

This is a work of fiction.
Names, characters, places and incidents originate from the writer's
imagination. Any resemblance to actual persons, living or dead, is
purely coincidental.

First Published in 2024

Olympia Publishers
Tallis House
2 Tallis Street
London
EC4Y 0AB

Printed in Great Britain

Dedication

I dedicate this book to my strong and powerful nieces, Margo and Emmeline.

Acknowledgements

Thank you to my family who keep me going and my sisters for lifting me higher.

LIVING WITH YOURSELF

ROMOLA

I had given it a form, a personality that walked beside me as a companion. It was supposed to be easier that way, as though naming it aloud would silence the darkness. Everyone was calling on their weaknesses, naming them as strengths or shouting them aloud to claim help. Social media was filled with other teenagers expressing anguish and struggle; it was normal now. Perhaps if I had done that, I wouldn't have needed to make it so real. But *we* didn't do that, no one in my family would ask for help. There were times I even considered giving it a name, but I simply settled for calling it my demon. After all, it tore up my life like a demon would. It wreaked havoc on my body, as it possessed every section until I exploded, and the consequences would overturn my entire life. This was what it was like to live with social anxiety. No, my demon wasn't socially anxious, that was where he played with me the most, toying with my confidence. My demon was much more fussy, picking only the strangest and most important moments to pull my life apart.

Life was a sequence, where every day was the same, only the pressures of exams and social affairs to keep it stirring. I often found myself staring at the calendar on my wall waiting for the days to move so that I could leave for college. It was one of those super cheesy calendars with motivational quotes for the pictures.

My gran always found them somewhere; in those shops where only grandparents shop for super embarrassing gifts. It was usually easier to hide them in my room; my drawers were full of butterfly scarfs or lipstick cases. The calendar was actually quite useful, so I kept it there to torment me daily.

As I scanned my room it quickly became clear that there was very little that resembled me there. The room was a jumble of the past ten years. For my tenth birthday my parents had the genius idea of taking me to Ikea. That's what life was like with them, always combining big occasions with *useful* trips. I didn't mind then; I didn't know any different. Centreing my higgledy room is the bunk bed I picked out during that trip. Simple and wooden, it's not too horrendous, except for the fact that no other sixteen-year-old still sleeps in a bunk bed.

I tugged a Tangle Teezer through my golden hair. It was shoulder-length and the colour of a Baywatch surfer, except that mine locked in tight ringlets that bounced in a circle surrounding my face. Aside from the fact that it was often the source of teasing at school, I actually loved my hair. I wasn't the type of person to be typically bullied, instead I was one of those in-between people who usually went through life un-scathed... or un-noticed. That wasn't to say I didn't get comments, but they were usually discreet. I had the type of figure that irritated people, the type of skinny that for some unknown reason entitled people to call me anorexic or bulimic, when in truth I had a high metabolism. The worst part was that I was always eating, because I was always hungry and with every bite I took in public I would watch others looking at me, wondering if they thought I was about to run to the toilets to throw up. Even if I were anorexic or bulimic, there would be no compassion.

I stared at my reflection in the mirror, imagining the

beautiful, tall, skinny beach babe that my composition could've made, but instead I could just see me. I was the super skinny, slightly frizzy, big-eyed mess staring back at me, smiling with acceptance.

"Are you going to the social on Friday?" Cally asked as I picked up the phone. We had been friends ever since the first day at Burley West Comprehensive. Every morning before the start of a new term we would call each other and make a game plan for the term. It would usually consist of her discussing how she would avoid the guy she had spent the last term snogging. Cally was the coolest person; unfortunately, I wasn't the only person who thought so. Occasionally I wondered why we were still friends, but I knew it was simply because I had gotten there first. By the time social hierarchy was founded, we had been through too much together for her to dis-own me. She was classy and crazy hot. It was that combination that would usually have made her an enemy to any living girl, except that she was just too friendly. Her smile was infectious, and she knew everyone by name – even those people who wished to be forgotten; those ones who sat alone reading or had no friends. She would talk to everyone. Every term she would jump friendship group in preparation for future networking. She was clever like that; everything she did was to benefit her future in some way, but she did it in a way that wouldn't deem her a 'user'. It was a privilege if she chose your group that term and she genuinely enjoyed meeting new people so it was never considered fake. It was one of the reasons I could never leave her side. I had no other real friends at school. All the guys knew this and all the guys in school wanted her. If you have ever seen the movie "The Duff"... I am Cally May's duff. She was my best friend and my protection from being bullied.

I scoffed, unsure if she was making a strange, unfunny joke, and half curious if she was truly oblivious. I had never been invited to 'The Social', not once in the past four years of school. I had no idea why she thought this would be any different.

"Tempting," I teased, but she remained inquisitive. "I'll think about it."

I couldn't tell her I was not invited. I wanted to laugh and say, '*No Cally, I'm considered a loser at school and would never be granted access to a social event of such prestige.*" But then again, there is no explaining to Cally, it's partly the reason she's great. Life is so un-serious with her – a blissful change from the erratic arguing at home. I was also still living under the illusion that she had no idea I was a social outcast and thought I could keep it that way a little longer. At home we were just *us*: the two girls who sat up chatting all night or spent every weekend sleeping over at each other's. Our parents had even become good friends and we'd go on family holidays together every summer. At school, I'm embarrassed to admit, I felt beneath her. I was not her equal and the entire school knew it.

"Have you heard there is a new boy starting BWC next week?" she continued. Immediately my ears began to burn, peeling back and opening wide to hear the gossip.

"Who is he?" I nudged, as if he'd ever be cute. It was a BWC law: No cute guys allowed, or if you are cute you must be horrible.

"Some guy that used to live here, a friend of Jed's."

It was confirmed. Jed Jennings was a total class-A 'dickhead'; this guy was going to be exactly the same.

"Ha, great." I snorted into the phone. "I can't believe you dated that prick."

"Don't, it was a moment of madness." Cally laughed, but we both knew it was more than that. It was a moment of weakness, perhaps the only weakness Cally had ever shown to the school.

The first day of a new year always played out the same. At the front gates students crowded on the wrong side, as groups re-connected before dispersing into the grounds. Ushered quickly by re-energised teachers who hadn't yet experienced the burn-out of a full year. BWC had approximately one thousand students that were divided into seven main social groups within five years and a sixth form. These groups were meant to define you and without one you were the school reject. Like most schools you had the typical groups: the art block crew; computer nerds; the hippie circle; active brainiacs; the standard brainiacs; the random clique that were so mismatched it worked, and the IT group. It was this chaotic order to a new year that made it so terrible. Without Cally there, I had no group to run to.

"Girl, you look insane!" she squealed, running behind me. "Your plaits look so great!"

I had tried a new hairstyle to christen the start of the final year. I wasn't planning on staying here for sixth form and had decided to make this year different to the five before. I wanted to leave BWC with a few memories that didn't simply involve Cally and myself binge eating over Netflix.

"Yay!" I grinned at her, thankful for the comment and relieved that she was there in time to walk through the gates with me. "You ready for this year?"

"I'm always ready, girl." She really was. If it were even possible, she looked better this year than any of the previous. Her hair had grown and hung just above the waist in endless wavy layers.

"Are you ready to rock this year?" She smiled at me; an understanding smile that made me certain she knew I was petrified.

I nodded.

The new guy wasn't there, but his presence was rippling through the assembly room in gossips. Within the first minute of taking seat I had already learnt that he was in sixth form and was completely head-over-heels gorgeous. I tried to remember what Cally had said about him being friends with Jed Jennings. I attempted desperately to cling to the idea that he was horrible and unworthy of my attention. I was adamant that I wouldn't listen in and join in with the frantic need to know more, that spread like wildfire. But it was all in vain, my demon found its calling and rippled anxiety to my stomach. Flushed with frenzied heat, I could feel my heart pounding at the prospect of a future. In the swooping of a moment I had created an illusion of my ideal guy and pinned my fictional romance to the whispering character that floated in the air. Like the room of girls around me, I was desperate to find out more about the potential crush that would soon grace BWC.

"Have you seen him?" Alice sniggered through the corridor. She was looking straight past me, to my taller sidekick. Alice was Jed Jennings' sister and the worst human on the planet. She had made my life hell before Cally became my saving grace and would still if she hadn't wanted to be Cally's friend so badly.

"No, what's he like?" Cally sniggered, shooting me a look to acknowledge my frustration at being in the same space as Alice.

"He's so dreamy. He's with Jed now, in the canteen. I'll obviously be spending a lot of time with him, as he's a family friend."

She shot a look directly at me as she spoke; there was something in her eyes that made me nervous. It was a warning or something more, almost as though my presence threatened her chances with him. I quickly looked away and shook off the ridiculous thought.

"Let's go!" Cally snapped as soon as Alice had moved on. "We need to see this."

Her eyes were wide, ready for her new conquest. I could feel my shoulders dip; who was I kidding? Cally flicked her hair, puffed her lips and pushed her chest forward. If there was ever anyone prepared for days like this, it was Cally May. She was born for first impressions.

I had often been told I talked too much. So much so that this moment went more quickly than I can recall. The entire scene was filled by my frantic ramblings as I followed Cally as she glided through the canteen; her hand raised in a princess wave as she made herself known. I was two paces behind clutching the latest school paper, laptop and a pile of workbooks; too busy ranting away to see her move. Had I been talking a little less, looking a little closer ahead or even walking parallel to Cally, I might've seen him coming. It all happened in a gigantic swoosh. First it was the sound of a gasp, then a shriek and finally I saw him coming at me from the corner of my eye. Blue, he was like a giant blue triangle with two eyes and large ears. I felt my body stiffen and mouth drop in an attempt to cry out but it was too late. In one fast swoop a giant rugby player crushed me viciously against the canteen seat. My eyes filled like a sand-timer from clear to faded to completely black and my consciousness sat beside me, as I lay transfixed by the dark. There was nothing, no sounds, no pictures and definitely no new guy.

"Romola, darling, open your eyes." Mum's plum-scented perfume clouded my nostrils. "Romy, please, angel, open your eyes now."

"Did they open yet?" As he spoke, dad's thick musky aftershave joined the new aroma of my hospital bed.

"Wait, you haven't given her a chance," Mum snapped. I could feel her scowling at him, my heart clenching slightly.

"Sorry, Michael, we shouldn't bicker, especially now."

I could hear the sound of his fingers gently tapping against her shoulder. If I'd lain there one second longer his hand might have lingered a second more, their eyes locked, and their troubles drifted out the room for eternity. I could've done it, if only the sickly scent of musky-plum and the clinical hospital ward hadn't consumed every section of my nostrils and filled up my entire air-supply.

"Reporting for duty." I coughed.

"Romola." Dad smiled. "Do you know where you are?"

For a second I had no idea, I had assumed hospital, but seeing dad's stress-free, joy-filled face made me doubt my existence on earth.

"Heaven?" I asked, with absolute sincerity.

They both looked at each other and laughed... maybe this really was heaven. A stricken look glazed over my face and I could feel nausea thickening in my throat. Was I in fact dead?

"No, sweet-heart," Mum said, finally acknowledging my genuine concern. "You've broken both your legs. You should've come round a long while ago but you wouldn't. You've been unconscious for three days now."

I looked down at my legs, both bandaged from ankle to

thigh, locked tight in thick casts. I tried to shift a little in my bed but nothing would move, every section of my body felt heavy.

"It's the painkillers," Dad remarked, noting the fear spread across my face. "It'll take a while until you feel fully in control of your body again, and those legs of yours are gonna be resting for a long while now."

"Can I come home?"

"Yes, angel," Mum said. "We just need to get your papers sorted for tomorrow and we'll set up camp in your room."

"Camp?" I asked.

"You're not going to be in school for a couple of weeks until it's all a bit more manageable. But you were lucky, it could've been much worse with the weight of that boy and the position of the metal chair. I do not understand these teenage boys and their gym bodies." She trailed off in a maternal rant. "Anyway, we'll get your classwork forwarded to home for now, I know its final year."

My eyes began to glisten, making it impossible to prevent a grin from creeping across my face. Forget final year, a few weeks off school was going to be a dream.

ALEXANDER

They say everyone returns to their hometown at some point. It could be at the end of studying, or to settle down with a family. I never imagined I would be heading back there now, whilst at college. Yet, as we drove out of the city, it was as if I no longer had a home. This place we were going to was somewhere in the past, and the city, well that was somewhere you could never feel fully at home. It was more of a pit stop before settling on the outskirts. But at least in the city, there was life. You could disappear with the masses and pretend you were alive. That was sure to be better than returning to the rural English countryside, where everyone would know each other, and I would know nothing.

My phone buzzed against my knee. I had turned it onto silent to dim the sound for the journey. I ignored it, but it buzzed again, over and over until the vibrating sound was too impossible to ignore.

"Are you going to answer that?" Mum insisted, nodding momentarily to my lap.

"It's just messages." I pulled it out and flashed the screen at her; the consistency of the buzzing was making the illusion of a call.

"Still, they seem desperate."

I shrugged my shoulders and stared out the window as the towering buildings replaced themselves with billowing trees. There was something petrifying about the openness of green fields, like being lost in an endless emptiness. I was really not going to do well in the countryside. I looked down and turned my phone off as it began to buzz again.

I had ended my relationship with Elle yesterday. It was cruel, but it felt ridiculous to continue it when we were miles away from each other. Besides, things with her were intense. Not in the sort of way that you talk deep and share too much, too soon. It was intense in the needy kind of way, that meant she wouldn't accept that it was finished.

In city schools your options are limited. You can choose the simple option of invisibility. Sure, you might get bullied and I am in no way saying that lightly, but you maintain dignity. Whilst you are the school reject or class nerd you are saved somewhat by the fact that you are yourself. The other option is you can act. Acting begins like a challenge. Everyday you push on a face, be the strong, confident guy that attracts the girls and gets on with the lads. Until one day you don't have to try any more and the gap between what was real or fake fades. That was who I was every day. The shitty thing is, it wasn't me. In fact, it was so unlike me, I had no idea who I was. But it's what I was good at.

"Have you spoken to your dad?" Mum asked, clearing her throat a little. I can't help wonder how long she'd wanted to ask me.

"Um. Yeah. This morning."

She didn't ask any more. I just watched her for a while; she was practising her yoga breathing. Sometimes I found myself watching her the entire time, worried that she would forget to release the breath. It seems to be something that happens to women as they progress in life, a tick in the 'must try yoga' box. Her throat thickened, she began taking quicker, deeper breaths until she was almost panting. I grabbed her hand, clasping it tight into mine before the cries could turn into sobs. Neither of us spoke. This wasn't unusual, so it was best to just hold her until she could find herself again.

"Are you looking forward to seeing your friends?" Mum asked, taking a deep breath and placing her hand back to the wheel.

"Uh, sure."

It seemed that she took comfort in the idea that I knew people there. A consolation to the idea that she was pulling me away from everything I knew. I watched the fields lengthen and trees gather before us. The English countryside never seemed to change. There were sections of it that disappeared; replaced with built-up estates or roads. But as you looked into a small section of undisrupted land, it was timeless. The wide oak trees that looked as through they cradled a door to another world, stood tall in almost every field. Symmetry echoed as they were evenly divided into neat rectangles. Yet even in their order, the irregularity of their size created a subtle chaos, the English character.

"It's quite different isn't it?" Mum sighed, as though the weight of the last few years was peeling off her with every mile that took us further from the city. She had never enjoyed the city, we had only moved there for dad's work.

"It's different," I replied, unsure what to make of it.

Memories of a childhood rushed back to me with every passing field. Adventures climbing hay bales and building dens were in every section of this area. In fact, had I been returning only a few years prior, I know I would've been filled with excitement at the prospect of the freedom that could be found here. In truth I was glad to leave the city behind. I didn't particularly like it there. It was the space here that shifted me.

Everywhere was so open, so exposed. In all the vastness of the landscape I could be seen more clearly here. There was no hiding, anything could be revealed and I wasn't ready for that.

We'd moved into a house a few doors up from where we used to live. It felt weird. Everything felt weird. The layout was identical to the modern bricked place we were in before. It was a new-build then.

"Some of your things are upstairs. You should go up and have a look at your room," Mum said, balancing a few boxes and a lamp as she scrambled the keys in the door. I tried to help her as everything swayed forward, but I was too late and the doorframe caught the boxes. We both laughed a little, that knowing kind of laugh that happens when you foresee the mess you would've spent the next few minutes cleaning.

"Sure, I'll check it out and then help you with the rest?" I said with fake enthusiasm that seemed to be sufficient for her.

Walking in the hallway to this replica of the past, it was as though time had cut out the inner years of my existence. For a moment I imagined dad rushing around the corner, arms wide as I ran to him eagerly. I cowered slightly at the thought, turning to mum who seemed to be imagining a similar picture. She sighed one of her lengthy sighs, pushing the boxes onto the floor before retreating to the car. I knew she was crying; she always rushed away when she could no longer hold it in. Looking around the familiar space, the joyful memories of playing with dad were clouded by the more regular images of Mum rushing into rooms. She had always assumed I wouldn't know, that I couldn't see her, so I was ignorant to her sadness. I pretended not to hear the harrowing sobs that echoed through the empty house. Or to not notice the patchy foundation stains on her jumper sleeve or gaps on her cheeks from the faded make-up. I pretended I didn't see, but we both knew from the guilt-ridden face that followed her around for a week after.

I traipsed the staircase to the familiar landing and into the identical bedroom. She had given me the same room as before. It felt good to laugh. It felt real. Standing in the same spot I had stood in years before, holding bags of my belongings like I did then, I forced the laughter into a roar.

"ALEX?" Mum shouted, concerned from the floor below. I could hear her rushing up the stairs, taking them two steps at a time. "What's wrong?"

Fear and confusion spread across her face; she hadn't heard me laugh for years. I imagined myself in her eyes, a joker-like expression plastered over my face. I couldn't respond; the laughter had consumed me. She scanned the room for clues, finally relaxing as she knowingly made the connection.

"Do you want to swap rooms?"

As she spoke, she burst into a mimicking cackle, and we were uncontrollably laughing at the sad state of our life.

"This is going to be good for us, isn't it?" I chuckled, putting my arm around her and pulling her into me. She sighed, but this time it was a release. Everything was changing and although it looked identical, the past couldn't be re-lived, and we knew that now.

ROMOLA

This dream quickly became a nightmare. My entire body was motionless, with two huge legs glued to the bed. Having spent a day staring at the three walls of my room, I decided I needed to re-decorate. Dad rushed home before I came out of hospital and dug the sofa bed out of the garage; my bunk bed was not ideal for someone who couldn't walk, let alone climb. I hadn't had a chance to tell them they could chuck the entire unit, so the sofa slotted neatly under the bed frame. It created a little cave to hide in, so I chose to embrace the situation and bring out the inner child fort-builder in me. After all, no one would ever see the inside of Romola Herbert's bedroom, so there really was no cause for concern. It was paradise for three hours as I lay next to my laptop, binging through Netflix programs. But I have never been someone who could properly binge. Three episodes into a series and I'd be aching to run around the block of houses and re-fill my lungs with oxygen. Running was definitely not an option, so I just lay there willing something great to happen. I started small, staring at my bookshelf, attempting to will a book to my lap and unlock the Matilda power within. Eventually I took to YouTube, watching motivational videos on perception and the laws of attraction. For a day, Netflix, YouTube and TED talks were enough to entertain me. It was that blissful reset that everyone dreams of having. I was in absolute heaven.

If it weren't so soon after taking a six-week summer holiday I might've lasted past the day. Perhaps if I weren't alone, I might've lasted at least until the companion and myself drove each other to madness. This was all fictional. A little writing in my diary, a tenth scroll over social media, twenty-sixth scan of Instagram and my sanity had peaked by 10.04 a.m. on the second day of being housebound. I had reached absolute, optimum boredom. I was so bored, so still, so dead, that I may as well have been a corpse or a photograph or Alice Jennings; BWC's popular girl who spends her life in the same seats every break. I even found myself imagining I was Alice, which was something I vowed never to do. In this moment of insanity, I pictured what it might be like to be watched in desire or fear. I wondered how it felt to feel indestructible. This was fleeting; as soon as I imagined myself as her, I wanted to pull myself out of her shoes and throw them at myself for giving her my time. None of it changed the fact that I had literally nothing to do, other than Maths work, and who wants to do that when they're stuck indoors with an illness, let alone EVER!

"Muuuum," I began. "Muummm."

At the start they both rushed in, desperate to help, willing to be at my beck and call.

"Daddddd," I shouted, two minutes later.

Ten minutes later. "Mummmmmm?"

"What?" she shouted back. I was a little startled at how quickly she dismissed sympathy, but I knew how annoying I was. Each time she came, all I said was, "Hi."

I was just so bored.

I slept through the entire day three.

Over a week had passed and I was still confined to my bedroom, although I had learnt to handle it more now. I couldn't move from my bed, but I made a plan each day of what I wanted to get done and dad would pile it around me each morning. This usually consisted of books to read, paper and paints, bedroom drawers to organise or my laptop where I researched and wrote articles for the school paper. No one ever read it, but I finally had the time to dedicate to it. Writing had always been my place of escape, where I could zone out from the world or share the sections of the universe that no one would ever ask me about. I posted a new article online everyday and spent the afternoon researching the next. My bed had become the school editor's station.

One of the perks of having a bedroom on the ground floor is I can sneak home late at night and no one would ever know, but then again this would depend on me actually being invited to a 'social'. It's also great to avoid the heated flames of my parents arguing when they really get going. I think they feel that the floors are soundproofed because whenever things get heated they both head upstairs and start shouting about something as though the house were a sound vacuum. I have no idea what it is they argue about anymore. When it all began I would stand there and listen, choose someone to defend and lash into the other person with him or her. Eventually, I realised they had no idea I was even there and the things they were arguing over were so trivial, I really had no side in the matter at all. When they eventually began taking it onto the upstairs landing, (one person always in the bathroom and one half way into their bedroom) I was grateful for the reason to escape to my room. I would listen to The Smiths "Please, Please, Please let me get what I want". Sometimes I listened to it and laughed, as Mum and Dad both demanded they got their own way. Other times I pushed the headphones in tight to block out the sound.

"Romola, we have guests today. Would you like to join us in the living room? Michael will carry you through?" Mum asked, a few hours after breakfast.

"Um, no thanks," I finally replied to Mum. "I've got classwork to do."

She shut the door behind her, without questioning the fact that I would rather do classwork than spend a second in the close vicinity of her friends.

I began writing an article about 'the laws of attraction' after getting sufficiently inspired by Jim Carrey's successful story of visualising and obtaining a cheque. I always heard the cars first, my bedroom windows looking over the drive. I had grown to know the sound of Mum and Dad's cars by the grumble of their engine. A few close friends and family had also made the cut, but this car was unfamiliar. I listened closely as two doors opened and shut, as footsteps made their way to the front door. My stomach turned slightly in anticipation. I had perhaps stayed up too late watching Riverdale and got myself psyched in suspense, but my heart began pounding. Mum's excitement sounded before the doorbell rang, as her bouncing footsteps raced theirs to the door.

"Anna!" Mum squealed as she opened the door.

A squeal sounded in reply and everything was silent for a short while as the friends trapped each other in an embrace. I shifted in my bed. Mum had no friends called Anna that I knew and the sound of her excitement made me all the more curious. "And Alexander!" she squealed in an even higher voice. "Look how you've grown."

Heat rushed to my face faster than he could reply.

"Ha, yeah I'm definitely taller than the last time I was here."

Everything in my body froze.

"How are you and Michael?" he asked, like a polite and well-mannered boy would; exactly what Lex was not.

"We're good." Surprise sounded in her voice, as she spoke with a strange confidence considering their most recent daily arguments. "Come on in. Let's get some tea on."

I didn't know Anna and *Alexander*. I knew Anna and *Lex*, the Lexatron, the most irritating son of a family friend who made my young life living hell. Obsessed with Transformers, he was the seven-year-old that would tease me non-stop all day long. He would pull my hair, put mud in my toys and laugh at me when I messed up. He was the worst part of every childhood memory and yet my family loved him. Anna on the other hand was a second mum before they moved; she was my mum's best friend from their college years. I couldn't believe they were there.

"How's the move going?" Mum asked when they had seated themselves in the living room. Another benefit/disadvantage of a downstairs room, I could hear everything!

"Great," Anna replied. "Alex is a god-send, he's pretty much put the entire downstairs house together in one day."

I scoffed aloud at thought of the snotty Lexatron getting his gold star.

"Amazing." Mum gasped glee-fully. "What a charmer you are, Alexander."

He laughed a little and I rejoiced internally at his embarrassment. I had miscalculated the sound of my snort and silence echoed across the house as they all acknowledged my remark. Alexander laughed louder now and I could feel his glare through the walls. His laugh was different, not like the high-pitched squeak of the Lexatron; it was deep and sent a gentle vibration that burnt my stomach.

"How is Romola?" he asked, his voice completely new.

"She's doing a bit better now, thank you," Mum replied.

"Poor little thing," Anna remarked; I just want to give her a big squeeze.

Mum laughed aloud.

"She's not quite so little any more, Anna. Besides, I'm beginning to feel a little bit more sorry for Michael and myself. That girl sure knows how to demand attention."

I cowered down as they all laughed. Parents were the worst at spouting humiliating remarks without regard for the consequences. All I could hear was Lex's laugh.

I'd fallen asleep in the weirdest position. This was the problem with having your legs bound into casts, they don't move, so your body has to get comfortable around them. I didn't hear the first knock, just the lingering echo that suggested it had happened. Another knock.

"YES!" I shouted, licking my lips to dry the dribble that had dropped down my chin. Yuck.

"Romola Herbert," a strange voice replied, opening the door. I could feel myself drifting back into sleep. "This room really hasn't changed one bit, except that bunk bed. That wasn't there and the sofa bed of course."

I knew exactly who was in my room but I couldn't open my eyes. I didn't want to see him, I hated him and I couldn't bare to see the reality of my bed-head, drooling mouth and sleepy eyes. It was all too much ammunition for his fresh book of Romola mockery. I kept myself ridged, pretending to have fallen back to sleep, but he didn't leave. Instead he drifted through my room, picking things up and laughing. I was furious. I opened my eyes just enough to see him a little, but was sure to remain visually asleep. He was a tall dark blur. I shifted a little to be able to open one eye without him noticing. I could see him much clearer now and he was so different to the annoying Lexatron that would run into my room and trash it every day of the summer holidays. His black skin had darkened, his body lean and strong, dressed head-to-toe in black: skinny jeans, a t-shirt and leather jacket. The face that was once the bane of my life, chubby and snotty, had tight cheekbones; huge dark eyes and lips that made my stomach flip in circles. He was perfect. And then he laughed and he was annoying Lexatron again, enjoying my humiliation. I shut my eyes tight and waited until he left.

ALEXANDER

Her room hadn't changed. There were small parts of the room that were new, like pictures or additional books stacked unsafely on top of her already towering collection. Seven years later and it was like walking into a time capsule. As I walked around the space I couldn't help but laugh; there was something about it that made me want to scream. Almost as though she had kept it like that just for that moment, to remind me of something from before. In this glimpse of a moment everything made sense again. In there I was almost sure of who I was, or at least who I had been. I knew that was the space where I was going to unlock the past, just enough to figure out the future.

She shifted a little on her bed and I could see she looked uncomfortable, desperately trying to avoid me.

"I'll see you again then. Your mum just wanted me to check in on you, but we're leaving now."

She didn't reply; she just lay there in a jumble of blankets and tangled blonde ringlets.

I scanned the over-filled room and chuckled before retreating.

"Michael would love to see you, Alex," Sarah shouted as we began to pull away from the drive. "Will you visit again?"

"Definitely."

There was something about the old red brick house in front of me that was pulling me back to it.

ROMOLA

"I can't believe you're not coming." Cally sighed at the phone. It was our first FaceTime since the accident and I was desperate to tell her about Alexander. "It'll be so boring without you."

I laughed to myself. We had never attended the social together before, there was no reason for this to be any different. Except that this time she had a reason to use for me not being there, other than the one she chose to ignore every week prior; that I had not been invited.

"I've heard the new guy's coming," she squealed. "Alice said he'd be in her brother's year." I was a little startled that she hadn't introduced herself already, although I imagined my accident had interrupted it on the first day. I only then wondered if he had been there when it all happened, if he had seen it. Had he rushed to help me? What would he have thought when he saw it was me? Had he seen me?

Jed Jennings was Lex's accomplice and together they'd spent days plotting to ruin my life. This was when Alice was my best friend and things were completely different. Before people cared about appearances and social hierarchy. When we were young and still excited about the prospect of secondary school.

"Since when have you been speaking to Alice Jennings?" I snapped at the phone. A pang of jealousy shot into my voice before I could conceal it.

The only time Cally had ever experienced social unrest was

last year shortly after Jed dumped her. It didn't last long as it soon became clear that he was the one who would regret it. However, it was enough time for Alice to spread a rumour that didn't stick and for Cally and I to name her group 'The B*tch Squad'. They looked like they should be in Taylor Swift's girl squad but were far more bitchy and had been trying to claim Cally into their group for years. There was only ever one problem: me. Now that I wasn't on the scene, her fate was clearly sealed. Worst of all, she had clearly forgotten everything from last year.

"We share gym class and you know what I'm like at gym, it's much more fun to chat."

Cally hates anything athletic, but looks insane in her gym kit. It is the only class she doesn't take seriously which is why she is one of the cleverest girls in the school and second biggest book nerd; the first being me. I could read for England.

"There are twenty other people in gym with you and you had to talk to Queen B." I scoffed loudly. "Have you forgotten everything?"

I stared at her into the phone, trying desperately to force her to look at me.

"No, I haven't forgotten. It just doesn't mean so much to me anymore."

I stared at her viciously, but she refused to meet my eyes. The next few minutes were awkward.

"I know him," I snarled eventually. Attempting to shrug off my frustration and also use Alex to gain myself some points.

"REALLY?" she panted, looking up excited. "How come?"

How could Miss unpopular know anyone, let alone someone new to town.

"It's Alexander, a son of my mum's friend."

"Alexander, as in Lexatron, the boy you hate for humiliating you at your primary school?"

Within a second my momentary victory was defeated as Cally reminded me of why I hated him so much.

I was nine when I got my first period, the first in my year and the entire school. My fate, as an outsider, was decided from that exact moment. My entire body began to change and I entered a world completely unreal to my fellow classmates. Of course, my mum was so proud of her little girl, so keen to share the news that she overshared in front of Anna and Alexander. On his last day at school he rushed into my classroom and shouted, "Romola Herbert has her period," in front of the year group. He was taken to the headmaster's office, but it was too late, the worst had already been done. He was gone and I still had a year left at school.

"That's the one."

"Oh, Romy!" But I could hear a giggle in her voice. Nothing was ever serious to Cally.

That Friday evening felt different to any other. Even though I hadn't been invited, having my legs tied to the bed made me feel for the first time that I was missing out on something. I was tempted to get Dad to strap me to a crane and cart me all the way to the social in my bed, but I knew he would never do that. I couldn't understand the point in having a building company if I couldn't abuse it when I needed a crane. I attempted to pose the idea to him, but he just laughed. I suggested that I could sit on the outside, watching as the sixteen- to eighteen-year-olds snuck in beers and acted stupid. Although I had no idea if that even happened. I had no idea what happened at a social. Even in a crane, no one would notice me. But instead I remained in my sofa bed, pulling pages out of old books, scrunching them into balls and throwing them at the wall; I had initially attempted origami animals. As I lay staring at the wall I noticed the screen on my laptop light up, but I couldn't even be bothered to see what it was; I had reached a new level of boredom.

ALEXANDER

BWC was a smaller version of the school I was at in the city. It was cleaner, with more green areas and trees. Everyone seemed to know each other. If you didn't know someone, you knew their brother, sister, cousin, friend or they knew you. Your business was everyone's business. On the first day I knew it was a hundred times worse than the city.

"Just be yourself." Mum smiled at me on the way in. I felt nine again, staring in awe of my mum's confidence in me.

"Sure. It's cool," I shot back, giving her a perfect crystal white grin. *Who the fuck is that? Who am I?* I wanted to ask her, but she looked so proud, I couldn't bear to tell her about my teenage personality crisis. *Oh, hey, Mum, I know you're struggling with divorce, a new job and general life shit, but can you just let me know who I am? I seem to have lost him along the way.*

I whipped up my backpack and leather jacket and chucked them over my shoulder. BWC had a blazer uniform, I knew I wouldn't get away with the jacket but I had two choices. I could enter the doors in my blazer, smiling, charming... good. Everything I wished I could be. Or I could do what I was used to, I could fake my way into an easy school life, bad attitude and excellent grades. We'd arrived a little later as I had to register before class anyway. There were a few students still lurking in corners, but they were younger. They wouldn't know me yet. As soon as Mum left, I opened the door to the reception, took one step onto BWC's floor and yanked my blazer off and leather jacket on.

"Please wait here, someone will be with you shortly," the receptionist said, gesturing me towards the seats in the foyer. "You might want to lose that jacket too."

She was frowning slightly, as though my attire had already concluded her assessment of me. I wasn't surprised, I was used to it and it was the look I counted on. It was easier that way; being an immediate disappointment left very little room for actual failure. I pulled off the jacket and screwed it into my folded arm along with the blazer.

"Alexander. Welcome!" A man was walking toward me, with two arms wide and a beaming grin across his face. I was startled for a moment at the thought that he was going to rush forward and embrace me. His over-familiar countenance alarmed me that I should know him. "I'm the deputy head teacher here. Let's get you to class."

He introduced himself as Mr Franklin and it quickly became clear his friendliness was his approach to life. Every step he took was like a dance as he leapt through the corridor, his buoyance making me uncomfortable.

"This will be different to the school you are used to, I'm sure," he said proudly. "We're more like one big family here."

I nodded, whilst attempting to walk behind him a little to avoid his gleeful eye contact.

"Here, join into this English Lit class and your timetable will tell you where to go next. Off you go."

He gestured dismissively as we reached a classroom at the top floor of the English block. There was something to his manner that made it clear he could switch his mood quickly given the necessity.

I slid into the back of the class and into the seat clearly reserved for me by Jed who beckoned me towards him.

"Sit down quietly please, Alexander," Miss Pringle called, attempting to quiet the lively class as she spoke. It was all in vain; as I sat down all eyes were on me and there was no avoiding it.

"S'up, mate." Jed grinned, nudging me.

"S'up."

The rest of the morning was much like English Lit. Everywhere I went, new people introduced themselves to me, random students called my name in the corridor, nodding as I passed. News of my arrival had spread around the school like a virus. Even the teachers stopped to take note as they saw me, introducing themselves and their role as they did. I was almost grateful for the distraction that was building in the canteen at lunch. Almost… until I realised what it was.

The school canteen was crowded with groups from year seven to the upper sixth-form. It was absolute chaos, with some groups attempting to play music, others desperate to read or talk and groups of guys lobbing a rugby ball back and forth across the room. All this was made worse by the eyes that were focused on me, the line of girls trying unsuccessfully to find reasons to visit the new kid. It all stopped when *they* walked in. Just for a moment, when the entire school seemed fixed on the longhaired brunette who looked like a younger Angelina Jolie. I might've ignored the entire thing and enjoyed the silence for a while had they not been heading toward me. It was as though the room parted to let them through. I watched them approach, almost ignorant of the smaller blonde girl behind her until the rugby ball slipped out of a guy's hands and the room sped up again. As he launched forward to grab the mischievous ball his balance fell and the loudest squeal filled the room with fear. No one moved as the most deadly screams began to ripple through the room.

"HELP!" the brunette screamed.

Within moments the entire room shook. One of the dinner ladies had called an ambulance and the teachers were moving everyone away from the crumpled girl who was passed out against the bench. Students filed out of the canteen, speechless. I didn't move; I just stared at the familiar figure in front of me. My insides turned and my head almost burst with panic.

"SHIT, that's Romola!" I shouted, trying to pave my way forward. It was like swimming in a current of people all forced to leave, but conflicted by fear. I attempted to push them aside to get to her but the bodies kept pulling me back. Every step I took forward dragged me further backwards. I could feel my throat thickening and my eyes clouding with confusion.

"MOVE!" I shouted at the unfamiliar faces that watched the new guy with curiosity.

"Alexander, you must leave," Miss Pringle insisted as I managed to wade closer. Romola's body cuddled around the bench as the brunette sobbed into her.

"I can't. I know her."

"I understand, but you must give space for the medical professionals."

"You don't understand," I began, but it was too late. The canteen filled with teachers who continued to push back any remaining students so the paramedics could get through. My vision was completely obscured. I felt helpless and desperate.

"MUM. You need to call Romola Herbert's parents," I panted

into the phone a few seconds later. "You need to call them now."

"Alexander, speak slowly."

"She's had an accident at school. You need to call them, Mum. She's being taken to hospital now. Do you hear me?"

"OKAY, ALEXANDER. I will now. I'll be with you shortly."

Within minutes she was gone, flown away in an air ambulance. The brunette had gone with her, but there was no chance I was getting onto that helicopter and it wasn't the right time to argue. All they knew about me was that I was the new kid. They had no idea who I really was. As I waited outside the front gates for Mum to arrive I couldn't believe the events that had occurred. It was surreal that this was my first day at a new school; it was surreal that it was Romola. Nothing about this was right, especially the fact that I hadn't driven to school and was helpless waiting for Mum to arrive.

Waiting in the hospital was like waiting for a jury to decide the fate of the innocent. Romola's parents were there before we arrived. In turn they hugged Mum and thanked us both for our fast information, but they were barely functional. I'm not sure they even knew who we were. They just stared blankly at the room in front of them as if they could quicken the verdict with their glare.

"Here's some water, Cally," Miss Pringle whispered to the tall brunette crumpled on a seat in the corner. "Try to drink something."

The girl wouldn't look up. Silent tears kept falling from her face as she attempted to sip.

"Mr Herbert. Mrs Herbert." A doctor came into the room a

little while later, holding a clipboard, with a gentle smile. "She's okay. We had to run some tests and scans to ensure the injury hadn't effected her spine, however it has been contained to her legs."

"CAN WE SEE HER?" Mrs Herbert sobbed. Unable to contain her tears any longer they swept down each cheek with force.

"You can, although I must warn you she isn't awake. Her legs are badly injured; we have bound them for support. I can't promise you that she will be up and walking anytime soon. She is incredibly lucky the impact was reserved to her lower body, however the angle and force didn't provide any cushion."

They were barely making sense of the doctor's words, Mr Herbert was desperately trying to scramble the information together, whilst Mrs Herbert's feet were already pacing towards the ward.

We waited in the hospital a few more hours, but there was nothing we could do. Her parents were waiting, white-faced beside their daughter. The fear of what they could've lost hadn't quite left them yet. They barely looked up when we were allowed into the ward to visit. Two polite smiles thanked us as we enquired further and offered our help. I left them for a while to get coffee and food, which was well received, but it was clear we were no longer needed.

"Please call me if you need anything at all," Mum said, hugging Sarah Herbert as we began to leave.

"Thank you, Anna."

The journey home was silent. Neither of us knew what to discuss. The lit streets were quickly replaced with dark roads and the sounds of cars began to fade. As I opened the window for some air, we were hit by the noises of the night. Owls cooed in the distance and the wind whispered through the fields.

"Are you okay?" Mum asked eventually. We were pulling into the housing estate, only a few streets from the house.

"Uh, yeah I'm fine." There wasn't anything else to feel. It was the strangest start to any school year and the most peculiar beginning to a new school, but all I could be was fine. Unlocking how I felt about today, would be giving access to a part of my mind I wasn't ready to open. I knew that I was very far from fine; I was more confused and afraid than I wanted to admit. In a weird way I felt responsible for the events that unfolded. Not because I had caused them, but my personality had. I was a representation of everything that was wrong with school. My character was the reason Romola was invisible today. Had she been more seen by everyone, she might not be strapped to a hospital bed. I knew this because in the canteen I knew her and yet I barely saw her. In that moment, like the rest of the room, my eyes were on Cally.

ROMOLA

Alexander Hayward sent you a friend request.

I didn't want to accept. Talking to Cally had made me so much angrier at what he had done to me. But I was also curious and there was only so much I could take from his profile picture.

Confirm.

For some reason I waited, pathetically staring at the screen. I waited for almost an hour, before eventually chucking my cushion at the laptop and retreating back into my book.

1.05 a.m.
  AH: Romola Herbert... Are you still pretending to sleep or are you sleeping this time?

My screen lit up again. I was struggling to sleep due to a dreadful cramp that had started in my left butt cheek.

1.20a.m.
  RH: If you haven't changed, then I'm pretending to sleep.

Alexander Herbert is typing...

1.25 a.m.

AH: *See you bright and early.*

1.26 a.m.
   RH: *WHAT? WHY?*

Alexander Herbert is offline.

What an absolutely pointless conversation. What did he mean by see you bright and early, I didn't ever want to see him again. One thing was absolutely clear; Alexander Hayward had not changed at all. Of this I was certain.

I had attempted to set a routine to my strange new life, but there was very little to motivate me in the mornings. It had never been my favourite time of day and now they were even worse. At six every morning, my parents would wake me with the rise in noise as they frantically dressed for the day. At seven I'd usually be woken again as they left for work; which was now followed by Mum rushing in to get me changed before they left. It was almost impossible to be a morning person in our house.

"Romola," Dad said, peering around my bedroom door. No knock of course, I mean what if I'd been butt-naked, Dad!

"Uhuh," I mumble without waking.

"Your mother and I have to head into the office today to do paperwork and see how things are running."

"Okay."

I attempted to go back to sleep, pushing my head further into the pillow to disappear.

"We have asked Alexander to come over and keep an eye on you whilst we are out. We really need to get a good day's work done."

Within seconds I was bright-eyed and wide-awake, my stomach quickly lined with acid. Dad was still talking but I had tuned out. Lex the Lexatron was BABYSITTING me! Could my life have gotten any worse?

"But, Dad!" It was no use; he was already half out of the door.

I felt sick all morning, but there was nothing I could do about it. Normally I'd be out of bed, running around my room or doing yoga. If that didn't work I'd read, but I couldn't reach any of the books. Mum had come in before they left to help me wash and change my t-shirt. I had been living in extra long t-shirts and underwear. I had nothing to do but wait. There is nothing worse for an anxious person than time. Time sits there mocking you as you desperately try to put some order in your nerves. Time slows itself when you are struggling, to prolong the torment. I was well acquainted with time because he always followed anxiety.

A little after they'd gone I heard the door unlock; heat pulsed from my stomach into my throat. *"What the hell, stomach, what are you playing at? It's only Lex."* But he didn't look like Lex – he looked hot as hell. I tried to forget it, but there was the teenage girl inside me who wouldn't let me.

He knocked twice.

I could hardly pretend to be asleep now. Panic shot through my body.

"Yes?" I tried to act normal, but my voice was crackly.

"Can I get you anything?" He opened the door and smiled as he peered in. Everything about him looked different. I couldn't speak.

"Uhm." My voice began to break. "I'm okay." I couldn't look at him as I spoke, a weird nervousness flushed over me at the realisation that a seventeen-year-old boy was at my door talking to me and I was in my knickers.

"Cool." He smiled again, his teeth a perfect white. "Give me a shout if you want me."

The words "want me" rang over in my head. Over and over, until I shivered myself back into the room.

It felt strange; I was burning with heat, embarrassment colouring my skin red. But why? It was only the snotty Lexatron. Wasn't it?

ALEXANDER

Walking around someone else's house is always weird, but this was surreal. I'd spent so much time here in the past. I'd even brought friends over here. It was like a second home that I hadn't been to in a very long time. Only it wasn't close family here any more, but a distant one that once was close.

The walls were covered with her photos, a clear reminder that Romola was an only child. Except for the younger ones with me in them, which were almost half. It was strange seeing that boy; was that the real me? I couldn't decide if I was still that important to the Herberts or if they hadn't redecorated since we moved. Nothing else looked different here, except Romola. The pictures of her now were so different.

I walked into the kitchen and poured a glass of water. Even the glasses were the same.

I pulled out my laptop and attempted my English Lit coursework. I liked studying. It wasn't the information I enjoyed, but the personality attached to studying. The thought of being someone who thinks bigger than what is in front them. I could be an absolute loser at school but if I could pass a test that was one area I wouldn't suck at. It also gave me a chance to avoid people. No one could hate on you for swatting in the library if you were a bad ass the rest of the time. Studying was my utopia.

ROMOLA

OH NO!

I called Dad immediately.

"What is it, Romola?" Mum answered.

"Dad's not here."

"Yes, I know." She seemed annoyed, busy and distracted. "He's here with me, Romola, you know that."

Her voice sounded strange, but I ignored it.

"Of course I know that... but I need a wee!"

The phone went quiet. He'd been carrying me to the toilet all week, propping my legs on a chair and waiting outside for me. I could hardly ask Lex to do that. As soon as I thought it, I could hear my mum say it.

"I'm sorry, Romola. Can you ask Alexander?"

"MUM, NO!"

"He's matured a lot, he'll understand."

It wasn't him not understanding I was fearful of, it was the humiliation. I couldn't face another second of humiliation in front of Alexander Hayward.

"Please, Romola, we really have so much to sort here."

The conversation was over.

I waited twenty minutes before I knew a second later I would be in serious trouble.

"Alexander?" I whispered, hoping he wouldn't hear, but either he had super hearing or my walls really were paper-thin.

"What's up?" he called back from behind the door. I was half tempted to ignore it, but my bladder would've burst.

"Can you come in?" I mumbled.

Fully in front of me I could appreciate what he had become; every part of him was evolved. His chest was bursting with strength and eyes glistening with charisma. This was far more embarrassing than I had imagined. And then he smiled.

"Will you carry me to the bathroom please?" I couldn't look at him as I spoke, but could feel the redness forming on my face. I was one of those unfortunate girls who wore all their emotions on their face. He said nothing and lifted me close into his arms. They were so firm; I could feel every muscle pressed against my skin. My stomach churned.

"Romola Herbert, I think we've been here before." He looked straight into my eyes, smiling a gentle side smile. My stomach started burning and eyes began to water.

"We have?"

"Just before I left, you fell from the tree in the garden and I carried you inside."

"Only because you felt guilty you'd chased me up there in the first place," I taunted.

He laughed and I almost threw up.

"Give me a shout when you are done." He smiled. I could feel my face turning brighter red as I bit hard on my lip and tried to smile. When he left me alone on the toilet I shuffled my knickers down my legs, semi thankful for wearing my extra large, fully butt-covering pants and also wishing I owned something lacier on the odd chance something happened. I shook the thoughts out of my head and tried to be as fast as I could to get back into my room.

I paused for a while before calling him back. I wasn't ready to be carried again, but the longer I was in here, the worse he would think my toilet needs were. I wanted to spray the room with air freshener; Mum had bought a fancy brand that made the room smell like English woodlands. I couldn't use it, because again he would wonder why I needed it.

As he lent over to lift me this time I could smell the deep Shea scent of his skin. He was warm and soft against my arms. This time felt different, I was no longer bursting for the toilet, but I also felt weirdly okay. My stomach was calm. I could feel my cheeks touching my eyes as I tried hard not to smile.

"You seem different," I said quietly.

"Six years is a long time. People change." He laughed a little as he put me down on my bed again. "Though apparently not your bedroom," he said, coming in a little too close, my face flooded with heat again.

"How was last night?" I asked as he got up to leave. I didn't want to be alone again, but he quickly got the hint. Without hesitation he walked back and sat next to me on the bed. I shuffled, pulling my t-shirt down over my thighs a little too quickly; it pinged back up. Now I was fully thankfully for the granny-pants.

"Burley West social?"

I nodded, but wouldn't look at him; I had no idea who he was.

"Full of far too many guys chasing after girls and girls after guys. I'm sure it was no different to the last one you went to."

I looked at him; he wasn't teasing.

"Ha, yeah, probably."

"What's happened in the life of Romola Herbert since I've been gone?" He turned onto his side and looked directly into my eyes. My thoughts traced the strong line of his jaw, directly to his lips.

"Truth or fiction?" I managed to say.

He looked startled for a moment.

"Both." He grinned, intrigued.

"In the tales of Romola Herbert I became the most beautiful, amazing, popular teenager, who had a band of followers and guys that fell head first when they saw her." I flushed bright red as I realised what I had said, but he laughed, eyes wide.

"But of course she became the most intelligent and towards the end of high school, everybody worshiped her and every school wanted her."

"In truth," I continued, looking down and pulling the t-shirt between my fingers, "I am unpopular, unwanted and unable to move."

He laughed and lay back against my pillow. Who was this boy?

"Ha, that's morbid. Seriously, though, no one's unwanted." He smiled again, this time it was to the side, but he didn't look up. We stayed there in silence for a while.

"What about you, Lexatron?" I laughed.

He sat up again, a cheeky grin spreading across his face.

"Lexatron. I had almost forgotten."

What had I done? That childish face was once again staring back at me, ready to torment me.

ALEXANDER

I kept staring at her hair as it bounced around her face playfully. There was something menacing in her manner. She could trick the most confident people into doubting themselves with one glance, as though she could see through you to your darkest thoughts. I pushed myself back against her pillows; perhaps if I could fall behind her gaze, she wouldn't read me. Who was I kidding; even I couldn't see myself.

"Do you have a boyfriend?" I teased, watching her cheeks turn red instantly. They've always done that. I used to think it so funny; I'd shout really embarrassing things at her just to see them redden. One time during primary school I called her out in front of the entire assembly because she had toothpaste on her cheeks. She blushed so bad I felt her cheeks burn through to mine.

This time it wasn't funny, just sort of cute.

"Me?" She laughed, turning her head away, so that a curl fell across her cheek. I felt an urge to move it, but resisted.

"No. I don't have a boyfriend. Do you have a girlfriend at your old school?"

"Sort of." I could feel heat rising to my own cheeks; thank God for my melanin. "I was seeing a girl before I left, but it's pretty much done."

Saying it aloud I realised it really was over. I was stringing her along, to keep something back in the city. In truth I had strung her along throughout the "relationship" – it added to the douche disguise. Elle wasn't like your average "IT" girl, which made being around her more bearable, but me even worse. She was smart; she even joined me in the library, where we would study in silence together. Most of our time together was silent, studying, watching the guys goof around or making out. We spent eighty percent of the time making out.

Romola shuffled down against the pillow, her eyes focused on mine. We locked for a moment, until the moment passed and I freaked out that she could see me: the douche or the other me. I wasn't ready for anyone to see either.

"You need anything?" I asked, before sitting up and heading over to the door. I could see the confusion spread across her face, but I was used to that. It was the same face that stared back at my reflection.

"No, I'm okay," she replied.

"Okay, just give me a shout." I smiled, backing quickly out of the door like a convict about to be revealed.

ROMOLA

One thing about being bed-ridden, you have too much time on your hands and you decide to research. I use this word because it is the sort of stuff you would never, in a million years, look up if you actually had a life. For example, yesterday I learnt how to fold t-shirts via a YouTube channel, the result being two tall, identical towers of perfectly folded t-shirts. A pointless waste of time as by tomorrow they will be chucked on the floor. It was also a way to distract myself from thinking about Lex; but that is impossible. Even Cally had been driving me mad, not picking up the phone. I was convinced she'd joined the B*tch Squad. Welcome to my paranoid teenage mind.

"Romola," Mum shouted from the hall.

I debated ignoring her, but then I noticed a second voice.

"Yes?" I replied, too politely; I could hear Mum's confusion.

"Are you decent?"

What is wrong with parents, always having to be embarrassing? I went red even though there was a wall between my visitor and me. I hadn't seen him for a week, plenty of time for anxious thoughts to escalate and for me to over-evaluate everything.

"MUM! YES!"

She didn't reply, so I waited.

And waited.

He knocked once, before walking in.

"Come on, Romola, I'm kidnapping you."

"What do you mean?" I replied, watching as Lex grabbed my purse and phone and chucked it into his bag. I almost said *Hey, what are you doing?* But he seemed too determined to protest.

"We're going out."

He left the room, returning five minutes later with a wheel chair with leg rests.

"NO WAY! I'm not sitting in that." I burst out laughing; I couldn't hide my joy.

If I had thought the toilet scenario was intimate, that is because I hadn't foreseen this. Before being submitted to my personal *bedlam*, my interactions with boys were sparse. This was more physical male contact than my poor stomach had ever had to endure; I could already feel it filling with vomit. YES, I throw up when I like guys – like every day – until I decide I no longer like them. But I didn't like Lex like that, so I bit my lip and tried to persuade my stomach to stop freaking out.

"Where are we going?" I asked, as he propped a box under my legs in his car. He hadn't been driving for long, and was the first person I knew to have a car. I felt like royalty; but I didn't look like it. I caught a glance of myself in the car mirror. My hair was in that third-day state where it was beginning to look greasy; I scrunched it up into a messy bun to make the disaster look purposeful. That failed.

"Rock climbing." He sniggered.

"HAHA."

"You'll have to wait and see."

I couldn't be bothered to fight it; anywhere was better than my room.

In my lap my phone flashed:

Cally<3May added to their story for a first time in a while.

I felt jealous; Cally was on her Instagram and had completely ignored my past four days of messages. Worse than that, I knew what her post would be. I slid across the screen, trying to check the post without Lex noticing. My stomach danced with anger.

Cally<3May: *Who wore it best?*

Dressed up in period costumes on a drama trip to Stratford-upon-Avon, Cally and Alice Jennings (Queen B... Queen B*tch more like) were posing, arms linked, fake pouts and kisses for each other. I put my index finger into my mouth pretending to gag, completely forgetting where I was.

"I'm guessing they're not your favourite people?" He laughed, noticing the picture on my phone and my face expression.

"Yeah, something like that."

As I sat there I could feel my world changing, my body settled against the warmth of a new car; headed somewhere I had no idea of. I could hear the deep movements of Lex's breath, like a metronome sending me deeper into my contemplative state. I had no idea what I would be returning to at school. Who would I be? Where were my friends? Nothing felt certain any more, nothing other than this solid seat. But after a moment's deep contemplation my survival defences kicked in and comical Romy was back, laughing nervously.

"You are strange, Rome," Lex said, joining in with my hysterical laughing. I paused at the nickname 'Rome'. I quickly became aware of myself, but he was smiling so I continued to laugh.

A little while later the surroundings began to become more familiar. Small bungalows piled back against the edge of the road and dotted between them were small shops. The cars began to filter off the roads and greenery built up again; more houses, trees and then it hit us; the vast, steel blue ocean.

"YAY!" I shouted, forgetting myself. I hadn't been to the sea in years, since before things became bad at home.

As we got out of the car, neither of us really spoke, except a few comments from Lex to see if I was okay. I nodded, finally aware that we were about to spend the day together and were no longer the childish boy and girl forced to spend time together.

"Do you remember coming here?" he asked, locking his car and wheeling me down the ramp to the sand.

I nodded; a little embarrassed at the fact he was pushing me.

"You were so annoying." He laughed, breaking through my fears.

"EXCUSE ME!" I tried to look at him a little. "You were the one always throwing sand at me."

"I was pretty mean to you, wasn't I?" He grinned.

"Yes, you were," I replied, satisfied.

The air was cold, but the autumn sun shone over the water, sending ripples of silver across the surface. The beach was quiet, a few couples walking with dogs and children running into the sea, squealing as the waves chased them. There is something about the sea that fills you with emotion. I could've cried but had no reason to.

"Why did you move back?" I asked without hesitation, immediately wishing I hadn't. His voice hardened a little.

"My parents have separated."

I punched my fist into my stomach, as the thought of my parents separating stung at my organs. Each night I heard them argue I imagined them in different places; the house would either no longer exist or one of them no longer be in it; where would I be? I often had to shut my eyes and push the thought aside. Without my parents I had no certainty. I gulped in too much air as I tried to breathe in, encouraging a minor coughing fit.

"Are you okay?" he asked, thankful for the distraction; he clearly was also lost in thought.

Curiosity urged me to ask more; there was something about Lex that makes me feel like I need to know. I used to know everything about him – he was boring and predictable – now I knew nothing.

"Was it awful?"

He wheeled my chair into a cove, backed against the rocks so that all that was before us was water. I tilted my head slightly to catch sight of him. He was resting on a low rock, elbows touching on his knees staring at the endless sea. His jaw was moving. It had always done that when he was thinking; a nervous trait I used to hate. Noticing me watching, he bit his lip a little, tightening his cheekbone on one side.

"It was terrible." He turned to look directly at me. "It's like finding out your entire life was based on a lie. They had only stayed together because of me."

"You chose to move with your mum?" I persisted. He was clearly uncomfortable but selfishly I wanted to know. I needed to know what would happen to me if my parents split up.

"I didn't really care who I went with, it wasn't going to feel right with either of them," Lex said. "But Mum needs me."

"I'll race you to the sea," I said, desperate to change subject

before remembering I was in a wheelchair.
  "I think I'm gonna win," he sniggered.
  "Oops."
  Then he looked at me and I knew I was broken.

ALEXANDER

"S'up?" I blurted, fist-pounding Jed Jennings and each of the guys that crowded the table as I slid into the corner. This was where they spent lunchtimes, locked in the corner of the canteen. It was the best place to see everything, which was the reason they acquired it. BWC was exactly as I had anticipated. I was immediately grateful for knowing Jed Jennings as it soon became clear it was much worse than the city schools. With less to occupy their time, gossip became the sole purpose of recreation. Jed was my ticket to safety; there was no doubt about my position there, whilst Jed was on my side. The one thing I hadn't anticipated was that I was the only black guy in my year. I had entered the white suburbs. You could spot us instantly, the three of us that is. Jamal and Daliah were twins a couple of years below me. Complete opposites, they hung out on either side of the canteen, spreading the melanin across the space a little. Daliah wore her hair in the longest braids that even when tied in a high ponytail, they would sit just above her waist. Clearly one of the more popular year elevens, she was always surrounded by a swarm of guys and girls. She dressed like an army cadet, chunky pockets on army trousers and tight t-shirts paired with bomber jackets and boots. At school she tried desperately to replicate her image, trading her trousers for black khaki. The centre of the group, yet she always appeared distant, like she had placed herself there for convenience, but was in fact biding her time. She sat swaying slightly to her headphones and the music only she had access to. She gave no fucks and everyone knew it.

Jamal was less fortunate, or perhaps more so. He was your typical geek, but owned it like a gift. His section of the canteen was home to the rejects; small groups whose only interest in each other was the proximity of their tables. He had friends, only two, who spent their lunch with their heads in their laptops. Even though they were different, they were close. I knew this because I had met them already through my mum's church group that met every Sunday. They were the most peculiar pair who spoke in different languages, walked in different worlds but got on like they had no differences at all. I had expected to see them at BWC, but I hadn't expected them to be the only other black kids in school. Church group aside; we would've clocked each other within the first day, had it not been for Romola's accident.

"Hey, Alex, you coming to the game on Saturday?" Luke Gilmour called at me through a mouthful of baguette. He ate every meal as though he hadn't eaten for weeks, lettuce and bacon spilling from his lips as he chewed.

"Course he is," Jed answered for me. "Get you'self on the team, mate."

As I watched Daliah lost in her world of music and army clothes, and Jamal in his laptop, I considered what might've been had I not chosen this façade. I was impartial to football, yet there I was surrounded by the football team. I was actually pretty good at it. I had been playing for years, desperate to keep myself in the right groups. As Daliah flicked her braids off her shoulder I couldn't help but wonder what it felt like to know yourself.

"Yup. I'm down," my outer personality answered for me.

"SHHHHIIITT. It's Cally-May!" Luke spat his baguette across the table before attempting to hide behind it.

"Am I missing something?" I said, watching the girl from

the hospital parade across the canteen. I had seen her a few times since that day.

"Gilmour is in hell with this girl." Jed sniggered. "They dated for about a week last year. Which to be honest is probably her longest." He sniggered again. "He's been a sucker ever since."

"You dated her after that," Luke scoffed at Jed bitterly. Jed shrugged his shoulders and laughed.

"Ha, yeah, but I didn't get dumped."

"She's Romola's friend, right? I remember her from the accident." I regretted bringing her into this uncensored group the moment I spoke. There was nothing normal about these guys; even the girls they liked were torn to shreds in their conversations. I had no idea what they'd say about Romola. I wasn't proud to admit that I knew she wasn't exactly everyone's favourite.

"Ha, yeah, more like Granola. The super dork that hangs around with her," Gilmour spat. They all laughed.

I wanted to hit the prick. But I didn't.

"You know her?" I managed through gritted teeth, attempting to salvage something for her.

"Nobody knows her. She's a total freak, spends all her days writing the shitty school paper that we use to wipe our asses. The only thing we know about Granola is that her friend is super hot. So I guess she's got some uses."

I watched his cheeks spread to meet his ears in a sheepish grin. In that moment I could see him as kid, the type that made everyone feel indirectly bullied.

There was a guy like Luke at City High. Chris Green was the ultimate loner but had so much dirt on everyone; you'd be in constant fear he'd pick to target you. Sometimes the shit he'd find on you, you weren't even aware were problems, until it was chanted at you non-stop for a year. My time in Green's hot seat came in year seven, when I first arrived in the city. The target he used was "sheep lover" or "horse kisser". Neither true, but the mere fact that I came from the countryside left everyone enough curiosity for the words to have weight. That was when I left myself behind and conformed. At the start of year eight, I was gone and *Alexander Hayward* was the new untouchable. Green didn't stop with me; his favourite target was Etta Lee, a small geek that clung to her books in the corner of the canteen. He didn't particularly have 'dirt' on Etta Lee either; she did nothing to create gossip. It was much more primitive, he simply hated her for her appearance, cleverness and social awkwardness. Her presence was enough to infuriate him. It made everyone in the canteen wince as he spoke to her; silence would spread over the room in a ripple as he spoke. We were all too cowardly to stand up for her, until one day her space in the canteen was vacant.

Luke Gilmour was a popular, less vile version of Chris Green; given the opportunity I knew he'd make Romola his Etta Lee.

"I have no idea why you waste your time with them," Daliah said the following Sunday. "I mean, you don't even seem like the type of person to be in that group. Sure, you look the part." She scanned me up and down to clarify she meant my appearance. Daliah had no concern with boundaries; telling someone what she thought of them, good or bad, was just a passing comment for her. It's what made her so easy to talk to.

"Fuck knows," I replied.

"I mean, sure, it must be easier, everything comes easy to

them. But they are literally the worst."

I couldn't help thinking she was hypocritical. The group she chose to hang around with weren't exactly the school outcasts, but I knew what her reply would be because it was the same reply for everyone. No matter what group they had chosen to be in, it was normally because it was who they were. Daliah's group of popular hippies were her choice, because she could be one hundred percent herself, sit on the edge and listen to her music, wear what she chose and still belong with them. This was why I barely spoke.

"So, are you Christian?" I asked her, nodding towards the gathering of adults in the dining room. Her eyes went wide and she struggled to swallow the tortilla crisp she had loaded with dips.

"I mean, can I really answer that here?" She laughed, shaking her head towards her parents. "I'm pretty sure they'd kill me if I did."

"So I'm guessing that's a no?"

"I mean I don't know, I'm more spiritual. Like I'm not saying there isn't a God or that any of it isn't like, real. But I just think I lean more towards the side of energy and inner healing. What about you?"

Jamal had entered the kitchen, leaning on the counter to steal the dips from his sister.

"What are you guys talking about?"

"God." Daliah sniggered. "What else would we discuss here?"

Jamal shrugged, grabbing a crisp and dipping it as far into the guacamole as it could go, until the crisp shook with the unbalanced dip.

"So what's your answer?" Daliah insisted. "This is where

Jamal and I really split the nest, he's got so much faith."

Jamal didn't reply. I had a feeling this was a common conversation between the twins.

"You'd find more faith in a spliff, more like," he eventually scoffed. Daliah didn't object, she just rolled her eyes and stole the tortillas from Jamal's reach.

"Shit, you do that stuff?"

"I don't do it, but I have done it."

"You mean you've tried it more than once." Jamal shot, clearly disappointed in his sister.

"Fuck. At your age?" I asked. Daliah clearly didn't like this remark, sending a vicious scowl in my direction. It wasn't uncommon in the city; most students had tried something at that age. I had no interest in drugs at all, it bewildered me that anyone would choose to send their mind into confusion, mine was screwed enough as it was.

"Fuck you. I'm hardly a baby and we're basically the same age."

"Just act like one," Jamal poked, snatching the crisps back from his sister.

We all laughed.

"Honestly though, I don't have my shit together enough to even consider the idea of God. Sure, I've followed the religion with my parents, it's been Mum's saving grace recently. But the idea of anything beyond this is all a bit too much."

"Whoa, you're far too deep for the likes of Luke Gilmour." Daliah sniggered.

"That is something I can agree with you on." Jamal nodded towards his sister. "That prick has it coming to him big time."

Jamal's remark was loaded and I wanted to ask more but the volume in the dining room began to rise and it was clear the church group was ending.

I grabbed the remaining nachos and headed up to my bedroom. I had barely unpacked and everything was left in an orderly mess. Chucking the bowl of food onto my bed, I headed to my laptop to play some music. The one thing I knew about myself, was that I loved music and it really didn't matter what type. I could spend hours sat listening to Spotify, creating new playlists titled for each month. Downstairs I could hear Mum clearing up after the group. Usually I would've stayed down to help, or already cleared before her group ended. Guiltily I was enjoying hearing her downstairs and for that moment just feeling like a normal kid, doing fuck all to help. Yet even with this momentary liberation, I still felt like leaping up and helping her. The one place I couldn't be a dick-head was at home.

As I lay watching the ceiling, I couldn't help but re-play my conversation with the twins over in my head. We were the only kids that came to the church group, which made it easier to just chill. It shook me a little how sure of themselves they were. I wondered if I had just majorly screwed up and missed the window for self-discovery. The only place I felt closer to myself was with Romola and that felt unkind because I knew she was falling for me, whilst I felt nothing. I couldn't feel anything.

ROMOLA

It clouded in like a wave of hot mucus filling my throat. Then travelled down to my stomach, until every section of my body went heavy with tension.

"GO AWAYYYYYYYYYYYYY!" I screamed at myself in a compact mirror. My parents were used to my sudden outbursts, neither of them rushing in. I often wondered what they thought I was up to.

"Devil stomach, leave me alone." I whispered this time, still embarrassed by the reality that I was never able to like a guy without being consumed by anxiety the next day. It started out like a guilty grumble that sat in my stomach, patiently waiting for me to move on. The grumble was a sickness, tempting me to vomit but never fully exploding. This nervousness eventually developed into confirmed vomiting, as the years went on and the potential for intimacy came closer. Finally it settled on a full-blown physical manifestation of vomiting and fever every morning without fail, until I moved on. I've done all the research, read all the forums filled with teenagers who fall for guys and then get so consumed with venom in their stomach, the sickness turns to hate and they no longer like the guy they have pined for. We are like vampires feeding off our prey, ill from their poison, before abandoning them when we can bare it no longer. The teenagers aren't what scare me, it's the adults; the ones who have entered the rest of their life and still get consumed by the guilty fury when their heart flickers. These are the ones that throw me deeper into the abyss of hopelessness.

"WHY ME?" I shouted again, filled with anger as my stomach ruined my future with anyone – with LEX. Did I even care? I didn't know him yet, so why could it already wreak havoc?

I punched my pillow repetitively, it's something people always seem to do when they're angry, but I just felt stupid, still tense, with a deflated pillow.

Alexander Hayward sent you a message.

I felt sick again, this time it burnt upwards, channeling from my stomach to my throat.

"NO, please," I begged.

"MUMMMMMMMMMM? I NEED HELP!" I shouted, staring down at the vomit covering my bed covers. This is what it was like, living with myself.

ALEXANDER

"Oiy, Alex!" Joe yelled, throwing a football at me. "Wake up, mate, we're on in ten."

I quickly snapped the ball from the tall blonde running towards me, his shaggy hair bouncing across his face. Joe was the first person I had actually began to get along with. He was dating a girl at university, which seemed to make him see college as trivial.

"Sorry, mate!" I tried to pull myself out of my head. Nothing seemed to be making much sense here, I wasn't falling into the usual pattern of who I was supposed to be. Before moving here I was determined to just be like before, but that was before Romola, even before Daliah and Jamal, before Joe. There were too many things here, trying to pull me out of myself. I wasn't sure I was ready for that, or if I wanted that.

The football pitch was at the bottom of the school, inconveniently placed as far away from the changing rooms as possible. It was going to mean I had to run to make it to the match on time.

I finally reached the football pitch just as the game was beginning to start.

"Hi, Alex." I felt a pair of cold, thin fingers brush over my shoulder, making their way from one side to the other. "Have a good game."

It was Jed's sister Alice, her mouth spread into a grin tilted higher on one side. She was cute in that Lily Collins kind of way.

"Uh, thanks." I nodded.

"Think you've been baited," Joe teased as I joined him on the pitch. "I'd watch out though, she's toxic."

I laughed, shrugging as I watched her walk away.

"Hey, you," Alice called, jogging towards me after the match. BWC won 2-1, which apparently happens every time. They haven't lost a match for seven years. Mr Stevens takes the sport really seriously; he was semi-pro throughout his teens and early twenties and teaches like he's still in the game.

"Hi," I reply, half glancing at her whilst continuing to the changing rooms.

She caught up with me, gently jogging as I walked.

"Do you fancy a coffee later?" She giggled, flicking her hair to the other side of her face and pouting her lips into a forced smile. Was I stupid, she clearly was the hottest girl in school, I couldn't say no. Could I?

"Rain check?" I managed to fumble whilst downing a bottle of water.

"Tomorrow then." She smirked. "Pick me up at twelve."

She sprinted into the girls changing rooms, turning just before she entered the doors to flick her hair again.

I stood still a moment, staring at the school gym block, confused about how I ended up committed to going out with Alice Jennings, tomorrow.

I didn't bother changing after the match. There would be some sort of after-match event happening. The guys would be going for burgers, probably with Alice and her friends. I couldn't be bothered, plus I'd already told Alice I had plans today. I grabbed my sports bag and changed my football boots into my trainers. It was Saturday morning and I had no idea what to do with myself. This was the new normal. I ran home, diverting myself down different streets to re-acquaint myself with the neighbourhood. Five minutes in and I had to turn around; I'd found myself in the centre of a new housing complex that wasn't there before. It took two more wrong turns before I decided to give up on the time-wasting exploring and brave going home. In the City I was rarely home. I'd always be out with the lads or at a match or with Elle. Things with Mum and Dad got so bad at one point, I didn't come home for a week. I found myself crashing at Elle's, I even booked a couple of nights in a Travelodge when I couldn't bare that. I couldn't help but feel a little offended that I hadn't heard from Elle in weeks. I had stopped replying to her messages, so it was no surprise and yet something about it made me uneasy. This time it wasn't arguing parents that made me not want to go home, but an empty room and a free weekend. Being back in this town, where life was un-planned, it was becoming too clear that I was going to have to figure out who I was.

"Have you had lunch, Alexander?" Mum called as I walked through the door. Things for her seemed to have reached a new-found freedom since being back. This was her home for a long time, so it was like returning to a place before divorce. Within days I could see the life and hope returning to her cheeks.

"Uh, no I'm good thanks, Mum," I replied.

The worst thing about feeling like you are confused about who you are, is your family. They seem to know you, or at least a version of you, better than you know yourself. It was just the two of us for such a long time. Dad was always working late or off golfing with friends, we rarely saw him. Until I did the same, abandoning Mum for school friends and Elle. I couldn't let her see the idiot I had become.

I ran upstairs before she could speak, wincing at the act that I'd done so many times before, to avoid confrontation. This time it was different, I wasn't the school asshole yet. I was exposed. I couldn't bare her seeing me and knowing I was in a state of chaos. Especially when she seemed to be getting some life back. So this time I fled, but took comfort in the belief it was to let her breathe.

There was only one place I could bare going today. So I showered and went to Romola's.

ROMOLA

"You can't spend forever in bed," Lex moaned on the phone as I refused to come out with him. I couldn't see him yet; I wasn't ready to see his smile. I had fully transitioned into acceptance. My stomach was raw, my body frail and mind completely absorbed with him. There was no denying it; this was the worst anxiety I had ever experienced.

"It's not forever." I laughed.

"It's too long," he continued, moaning. "Life is for living. Let's go make sand angels at the beach again."

"You mean you make sand angels and I watch."

I took a large breath and held it for a while to avoid gulping back my nerves.

"Seize the day, Miss Herbert." I could hear his smile through the phone. This wasn't working; I felt ignited.

"I'm staying here today," I urged. "Go make sand angels and send me a picture."

"*Hmmm*, maybe," he replied, distracted. "I'll be back. Wait there."

"I can't move!" I raised my voice, amused, but it wasn't the accident this time; my entire body felt paralysed with fear. Nothing felt certain any more.

He hung up the phone without another word. I sat there perplexed. What was happening? I pulled at a ringlet and waited for the ping as it rose back towards the root. I was alive and aching. I picked up my notebook and began to write – anything that came into my head. My mind was over-flowing with energy; I could explode with hope.

"Did you wait?" a voice called through the door. I didn't reply, I'd fallen asleep; the voice was distant and surreal. "Rome? Are you there?" This time I woke.

"Hello?" I mumbled, eyes closed.

"Can I come in?" he asked.

"Lex?"

"Romola?"

I didn't reply again, still half asleep.

"Do you have other people you are expecting?" he joked.

"UHHH, okay, come in," I stuttered, after grabbing my compact mirror and wiping dribble from my cheek. Panic shot through me as I scanned the room in front of me. Stacks of old plates were piled on the table and dirty t-shirts sat at the end of my bed; I tried desperately to wriggle them onto the floor. But it was all too late; there was no salvaging my dignity now. My room shrank as he entered; everything became insignificant. My stomach clenched into a giant knot.

"I brought you the ocean." He grinned. "Are you ready?"

It was one of those phrases that should've made me cringe, except that he was taking the mick and I couldn't help smiling, my lips curled high into my temples.

"How?" I asked.

He began pulling items from his bag. First was a turquoise blanket that he laid at the foot of my bed, whilst he began shuffling through a pile of DVDs he'd collected.

"*Jaws?*" He laughed, noticing the horrified expression spread across my face.

I watched *The Ring* with Cally a couple of years ago and

couldn't go to the toilet without the door open for about two weeks. Mum and Dad freaked out that I was going to develop a UTI, peeing so quickly so that I could avoid the 'well' of the toilet. I was useless at horror movies.

"*Pirates, Blue Crush, Fool's Gold, Lilo and Stitch.*"

"You actually brought *Lilo and Stitch* with you?" I joked. From the corner of his eye he gave me a little glance before continuing down the list.

"You choose," he said. "I'll be back."

He left the room and I sat there perplexed. This was exactly what I had dreaded, spending time with him in close proximity. Now we were going to watch a movie together? I would one hundred per cent embarrass myself.

I slid *Pirates of the Caribbean* into the side of his laptop, waiting for it to load. Five minutes passed and he was nowhere, had he really brought me the sea and left? I felt so confused. His laptop was in my hands, with everything I'd ever wished to know about him inside. I stared at the screen for a few minutes before clicking out of the movie and onto the desktop. This was a huge invasion of his privacy, but I couldn't help it. What was I hoping to find anyway? I knew everything I needed to know about Lex. I quickly clicked back onto DVD player and slid into my cushions, ashamed of the consideration. Another ten minutes, the house door flung open and a strong smell of vinegar floated through the keyhole.

He knocked.

I adjusted myself again, grabbing my compact mirror, which I had barely ever used before these visits.

"YEP!" I croaked, more nervous now than before.

He was so chilled, chucking his body back against the cushions next to me. I watched him edge backwards, every movement made with such ease. I could never be so comfortable. My movements were like a timid child – afraid to put up their hand; they fidget and bounce until the moment has passed and they are left with a burn in their stomach.

"You better be hungry."

The thought of food made my stomach dance around. I was always hungry, but there was no way I could eat now. I nodded my head, watching his long arms weave around me, creating a picnic across my bed.

"You still vegetarian?" he asked.

"Yep."

"I remember you turning... I'm pretty sure that was my fault too?" he laughed, a little nervously this time.

"IT WAS!" I mocked anger. "You chucking meat at me. Telling me it was dead pig."

His face turned cold.

"SHIT, I was such a dick." He sighed, staring down at the food to avoid my face. I burst out laughing to soften the mood.

"Really you did me a favour, I'd never have learnt I was eating a real pig otherwise."

He slumped back again, smiling at me through a raised brow.

"Toughening you up."

"Good morning, Miss Herbert," his calm voice buzzed down the phone the following day. "I'll be over in five."

I had a feeling this would be a regular occurrence. He would call me saying he'd be over and I had to be ready or else he'd arrive and see me in my pyjamas. He'd left quickly after the movie yesterday, but that was partially because I had fallen asleep. I wasn't sleeping and there was something about knowing he was there that settled me for a while. There was no fear or anxiety to stir me, because it was already real.

"Okay," I gulped every time I replied.

"Today we're going to the zoo."

"Are you serious?" I laughed.

"Why not… we need to do something you can actually do. Besides, it's the weekend."

There was energy in his voice that gave me hope.

ALEXANDER

As soon as I hung up the phone I thought of Alice and her plan to go out.

9.14 a.m.
    AH: Hey. Can't do this morning... family stuff. Evening?

10.32 a.m.
    AJ: Pick me up at 7. XXO

I flicked the phone between my fingers, back and forth, careful not to let it fall. I felt weird. Part of me felt like an A-grade douche that'd just scored the hottest girl in school, effortlessly. I couldn't help but smirk at her reply. Everything at BWC was so easy, it was as though I had walked in for the part and been cast immediately. But there was something else there too, at the pit of my stomach growling in an unfamiliar place. I gulped at the large glass of water on my desk. If I could've drunk it fast enough or taken in a big enough sip I might've shifted the feeling. Instead it just lingered there for a while teasing me. It was guilt, but it wasn't mine. It was one of the many personalities that sought refuge in my confused mind. This was the one who needed Romola, the one desperate to get out. For this version of myself, the mere thought of dating Alice felt like a betrayal of Romola. Alice was her opposite, she was the worse part of me and Romola was the best. I felt like a prick to admit it, but I needed Romola.

She was how I was going to explore deeper into my psyche, she was the antidote for my insanity. I flicked open my laptop to search for the closest zoo. It was Bristol, an hour and a half away. In all the time we lived there I went once. It was the other side of the city to where we lived and nowhere near school. My parents had taken me when we first arrived; they'd set out to do a load of touristy things – trying to settle ourselves into the city. That soon stopped, the arguing started and outings became rare. It's strange but through years of arguing I didn't miss them being together, that stopped long ago; I simply missed them. It was like they'd both lost the part of them that joined them together. My parents were different to the people I grew up with. There were moments when I wondered if this was when I got so confused. My entire world was thrown up in the air and personalities were falling around like scattered money; it was difficult to know which to choose. I snapped the laptop shut a little too hard, so I had to lift it slightly to check I hadn't damage the screen. I took another swig of water, this time letting it linger in my throat a while to increase the impact of the gulp. It didn't help but hurt my throat a little with the force. I grabbed a hoodie from one of the boxes stacked under my window, catching a glimpse of myself in the glass reflection. There was something mischievous about the person staring back at me. I looked away, shaking it off whilst I slid into the black jacket.

"Are you okay?" Romola asked, breaking the long silence that filled the car. We'd been driving for thirty minutes. After all the formalities it seemed like there was nothing to say. Except that there was so much I could've said, it just felt strange. I wasn't sure why I was there. The lingering guilt in my stomach was a constant reminder that I wasn't there for her.

"Yeah," I replied. "Just thinking about my dad."

She nodded and gazed ahead without speaking.

I watched her move out of the corner of my eye, shifting every few seconds to re-adjust her position. Her hand was clutched tight to her stomach and eyes darting across the landscape, desperate to fix onto something. She was nervous.

A smirk flickered in the corner of my mouth, a slight pride at making her flustered.

"How are your folks?" I asked to break the tension.

"Messy."

She dipped her head down to avoid any eye contact.

"Its almost worse now that I'm constantly in my room. It's easier that way for them to forget I exist."

"Shit," I blurted, slightly sickened at the recollection of events in my family. "Parents can be so blind."

She laughed, looking up and catching my eye. Her hair was pulled back into a tight ponytail, small curls bouncing out around the hairline. She looked young, like time hadn't tested her. Her face had post-coma dew, like someone who hadn't known hardship or sorrow. I watched her in careful glances, cautious of the roads; I hadn't been driving for long. She was watching out of the window as the fields ran past us faster than we could meet them. Even with the fresh face and sweet innocence that danced around her childish aura, there was darkness to her. It was internal, hidden below the security of her shielded upbringing. This was hers, it was the sort of energy that lay beneath the surface, shredding at her slowly. I knew this, because I had it too.

There are places that never seem to change, usually monuments or remarkable buildings. Returning to my hometown was like returning the day after we had left; everything was still centred on the same town hall. Bristol zoo was much the same; it was like walking straight into a memory, except this time in a semi-adult body. We walked through the gift shop straight into the flamingo area, before heading down to the lions. It was all the same. I could almost see the younger version of myself marching on ahead, a big sheepish grin smacked across my face. I was always a sucker for days out – any reason to be outside actually; I guess I got that from Dad. Being there this time with Romola was so different; yet I felt closer to that crazy kid sprinting ahead to the lions, than I'd felt for years.

"What shall we see first?" I asked, watching her eyes smile as she took it all in.

"EVERYTHING!" She laughed, whilst being utterly serious.

"Haha, okay. Everything it is. Do you want the goofball tour?"

"I expect nothing less than super goof-balling." She grinned.

I regretted it the moment I said it. It was easy to swan around confidently, messing about in front of people when it was at school, or with the lads – even with Elle. I didn't give a fuck what they thought of 'me', so long as it made people laugh. With Romola I wanted to be stupid and funny to make her laugh, but had no idea where to even begin. She was my adjudicator. It was like I was a dorky kid that had never sat up properly in his life, but had just entered himself into the lead in the school play. I just needed time to figure out how to play it.

I looked at her grinning up at me expectantly and my knees began to shake.

What the fuck was happening to me?

"It's cool," she said eventually. "We can just see where we end up."

I could feel her watching me, she was so chilled and her face slightly puzzled. I knew she'd seen me then, really seen me, the guy between the douche and the other one. She had seen me juggling between my personalities.

"Can you see the lions?" she asked, moving on. "It looks like they must be hiding."

It took me a few moments to recollect myself from morbid embarrassment. I watched her wheeling herself towards the lions and within a second he was there with her. I wasn't ready for her to see him, but my hesitation had flicked me into automatic. His arms were resting against the glass, deep in some poetic verse. He was great at that, turning something simple into the most pretentious shit. Whizzing her around in the wheelchair, making her laugh. I could feel my temperature begin to rise, sweat sitting at the back of my neck. It was as though I was watching someone else act for me, trapped inside another person's body willing to do something else, to be someone else. Anyone else would've been better than this.

I shot glances around the zoo, nervously imagining my body physically morphing between personalities, thankful that they all had the same face. The worst part was that she was falling for it. Her eyes beaming, full smile flexed across her cheeks. She was sucked into the Alex confidence, the cool-kid act I was giving her, and I was shit scared that she would like him too much and I would never have a chance to be anyone else.

"What music do you listen to?" I asked her when we'd sat down with coffee. We sat on a small picnic bench, surrounded by large families and school groups. The zoo was always busy, regardless of time or day. It was easier now, to be still and I could finally separate myself from the guy I was before.

"You used to be into all sorts of soppy stuff – Disney celebrities wasn't it?" I teased, her face glowing red. I felt such a wicked comfort in her blushes; they relaxed me.

"Yeah, I was queen of Disney." She laughed. "I still love Taylor Swift too, but I'm a bit more cultured now."

"Yeah?"

"Yeah, it might sound strange but I love The Smiths. It's probably my dad's fault. I do like modern music too."

"The Smiths are great. Do you still sing everywhere you go?" I asked, watching her face go red again.

"Always," she replied.

I watched her turning her coffee cup around repeatedly in her fingers, staring down at the cup as it spun. She barely looked at me.

"Do you ever think about what we were like as kids?"

"What do you mean?" She looked up at me, confused.

"You know, just how things were so much easier then. Like coming here, it was always such a huge event and everything looked so bright and exciting."

I wasn't sure whether to continue.

"Now everything looks so grubby and I can't help but see how small the cages are and how unhappy the animals look."

She sat up straight, scanning the space around us. Her eyes travelled across the zoo, starting at the jumping children who were blissfully enjoying everything, to the over-flowing bins or faded children's rides. It was easy to stop here and still see the joy. She continued scanning the area, watching the animals around us make their way through the cages, watched by the human gaze.

"Yeah, I do get that," she replied. "It's definitely not the same any more. Nothing really is the same when you get older, is it? Things are much more complicated." She clenched at her stomach again as she spoke, this time taking a deep inhale before she continued.

"But I wouldn't want to go back. Would you?"

I paused for a moment, considering what she had said. So much of my attention had been put on who I used to be. I held on to the illusion that I knew myself as a child. He was always so sure. I wanted his certainty, but did I really want to be him?

"Nah, you are right! You sure wouldn't want me to go back to teasing you like that, would you?"

We both laughed.

ROMOLA

We hardly spoke on the way back. Something was different, he seemed different and it made me uneasy. The second I heard his car leave the drive it was as though my stomach burst. Tears flooded out of my eyes and vomit flew out of my mouth – thankfully into the bucket I had stored beside my bed. After five minutes of clearing my stomach and sobbing hopelessly to myself, I sat back against my wall and stared into the room around. This room was smothered in my possessions. There was no doubt that it was my life I was living, but I no longer wanted it. I didn't want to be this girl, the one that couldn't live like other teenagers. I wanted to be the girl that made out with every guy she saw, laughed her way through every conversation, and sobbed her eyes out through every break-up. I wanted to feel what it felt like to even have a break-up – a real one. I wanted to eat Ben and Jerry's and miss someone, not feel the relief that I felt when I ended it with someone. Usually the moment I've called off anything I can sit down and stomach ten meals at one time – making up for everything I had missed the entire relationship. I wanted to feel heartbroken so bad that I couldn't eat anything for days. I wanted to just feel something – anything – other than this empty sickness that prevented me from being anything more than friends. I looked around the filled room and hated myself. Yet it was undoubtedly clear that I was unwillingly falling for Lex and that my stomach was not amused.

ALEXANDER

It was 6.50 p.m. when I pulled up to Alice's house. She lived in a huge new-build on the other side of town. Most of the houses around here were piled into rows that swirled into each other like a maze. Alice's house was set apart from the others. The long front driveway was immaculate – no forgotten shovel or mislaid possession. It was perfectly groomed. I lingered in my car a while. I was early and uncertain whether to enter at all. At 6.55 p.m. I had no choice – Alice had seen me from her front window and was making her way towards the car. She was beaming, a little bounce in her step as she walked towards me – the school's new commodity.

"Hey," she said, almost singing as she climbed into the car seat.

In every action she assumed control of the things around her – placing her fingers slowly across the doorframe, winding down the window, even touching my arm.

"You all right?" I replied, watching her flick her eyelids and hair in unison. She smelt like warm vanilla. Everything about her was perfect. So perfect, it was like she would break if you creased her shirt.

"So where are we going?" she whispered as though we were in a car full of people. "I'm starving."

I started the car and headed down the road towards town. There were barely any food places here, mainly pubs and the odd family-run restaurant. Either way it would be intimate and surrounded by loads of people from school. This 'date' was going to be witnessed by a few and broadcast to everyone within a second… if it hadn't already been rumoured. Yet part of me didn't care… perhaps even enjoyed that fact.

We settled on a small Italian restaurant in town, run by the parents of one the guys on our football team. As we walked through the door the entire team were sat eating pizzas and raising the volume of the restaurant above the 'quiet family restaurant' threshold. None of the other customers seemed bothered; it gave the place a buzz that made it seem livelier. I was ready to retreat when I saw them, but Alice didn't seem to mind and they spotted me too soon.

"Alex, you joining?" Jed shouted through a mouthful of pizza before noticing his sister next to me.

"Not now, mate." I gestured to Alice and guided her forward, placing my hand on her shoulder. It felt good; it felt easy. He shrugged and turned away, re-joining the others. Alice flicked her hair and smiled over her shoulder, staring intently at me for a second. This felt familiar.

We barely spoke through the meal, but it wasn't awkward. It was normal; my limbs were stable and thoughts vacant. It was simple. I liked simple, not because I liked Alice but because it was easy. She checked her phone a couple of times through the meal and grinned whilst she gossiped about some of the customers that came in. I relaxed, stuffed my face with pizza and laughed like an idiot at her remarks.

"It's so great you're on the team now," she said, taking the smallest piece of pizza, which she had sliced neatly between her knife and fork.

"We can totally double date. I have loads of friends dating

your team-mates."

I nodded, taking another slice of pizza and folding it before I ate it.

"Also, there will be huge events this term, so we'll have to make plans for those."

She took out her diary, flicking slowly through the pages to mark us down. This was a business meeting and she was planning the future of our stale relationship, on the first date. I wished I cared, but I really didn't. In fact, I enjoyed being with her. It was just normal.

"Cally girl!" Alice shouted across to the Angelina look-a-like who had walked into the restaurant. She was headed towards the team, but re-tracked towards us when she heard Alice call.

"Hey." She giggled towards Alice. "Hi, I'm Cally." She nodded in my direction.

"Hey. You're Romola's friend, right?"

"Yeah! Sure. You know her, right?" she replied as though it was new to her.

"Uh, kind of, yeah." I shrugged. "Our parents are friends," I added, unnecessarily.

Alice and I walked towards the car in silence. She looked great. There was a confidence in her step that made her all the more attractive. She was the type of girl who knew exactly how to manipulate a situation and I knew that life at BWC would be so much easier with her.

"Are you and Romola close?" she eventually asked, as we approached the car.

"Uh." I didn't know how to answer. It wasn't that I didn't want to admit that I was, it was that I didn't want to ruin it. "No, not really."

I wanted to make things with Alice work out. She shifted in her seat a little; clearly I hadn't been as convincing as I thought. Without hesitation I moved closer, pulling her face towards mine as we kissed.

ROMOLA

I felt terrible; my anxiety had stuck itself in the pit of my stomach, burning constantly. It fuelled energy throughout my limbs that made me constantly want to move; to kick something. I was an emotionally over-charged battery ready to explode. It had been a week since I spoke to Alexander. I had thought the break would give me time to settle, but my mind was confused.

"Hey GIRL!" Cally whistled, dancing around my room. "How's life?" Her ease annoyed me, like... *HELLO, are you serious? I'm stuck in my room!* She looked amazing; her hair waved against her back and her make-up had been done so perfectly it almost looked natural.

"Shitty," I replied, staring at my own reflection in the mirror. Mum had put a floor-length mirror in front of my bed – her effort to encourage me to get dressed – but it just freaked me out when I woke in the middle of the night.

"OH, HUN." She tilted her head sympathetically before dismissing the subject. "So you missed the best trip EVER."

She was different; as I watched her grace my room with energy, I could feel the heat in my cheeks. Her mouth moved up and down, but I ignored everything she said. I couldn't hear her through the screaming in my own head.

"Alice and I were laughing so much... "

Catching Queen B*tch's name made me overspill, I laughed a loud spit. She stopped a moment, staring confused at me.

"Sorry, my back was a little ridged," I lied. After all, how could I hate Cally? Her fairy temperament was the reason I loved her so much.

She shrugged her shoulders and continued.

"Oh, I saw Alex, yesterday."

His name fluttered in my stomach as she spoke.

"Really?" I replied trying to act casual.

"Yeah he was with—" she paused, watching me carefully for the first time since she had arrived. "Oh, never mind."

I wanted to know, but I was also desperate not to seem too eager, so I brushed it off.

"Anyway, you have missed so much!"

Twenty minutes passed and I hadn't said a word. Alice's name had been spoken more times in those minutes than I'd ever heard in my entire life. In the frantic business that had become my bedroom, I felt more alone than ever. I stared down at the newly changed bed sheets. Mum had refreshed my bed this morning, after I had been caught in a fit of cold sweats last night. As I stared at the prepared sick bin beside my bed and the piles of used tissues in my waste bin, I hated Cally. She had hardly visited since I remained at home, hardly even called. We had always been together through everything, yet now, when the worst had happened to me, she wasn't there. I hated her even more than Alice Queen B*tch Jennings.

"Why don't you just go back to the B*tch Squad, Cally? I don't need your pity-visit and boring antics. Go flick your Pantene-fake hair for someone who gives a fuck."

I bit at my lips as I shouted. I was so loud; all my fury at the past few weeks was spilling out and I couldn't control it. She stopped still in her tracks. Her face went solid and I realised she'd never been spoken to like that. EVER. Her parents were major

Cally pushovers, sucking up to her every whim, and schoolmates loved her. Un-prepared for the comment, she had nothing to say. She grabbed her bag and was gone. I didn't regret it; it actually felt great. Even with her gone, I continued screaming for the next five minutes. Anything that I could think of, I screamed it as loud as I could.

My phone flashed again:
Alexander Hayward sent you a message.

"Are we okay?" he spoke cautiously into the phone. I had ignored his messages for the past day. Eventually he called me on the house phone, so I couldn't ignore him. I could hear the phone getting closer as Dad chatted to him for twenty minutes, before finally bringing it to me. The entire time they spoke my insides worked on filling with heat and spinning around.

"Yeah, we're fine," I replied bitterly.

"Did you get my messages?" he urged. His voice was a little desperate and it made me smile.

"Uh, yeah, sorry. I've not been feeling great. Mum thinks it's the painkillers I've been given," I lied, easily. I had no idea what Mum really thought.

"Oh shit, yeah I forgot you'd be dealing with so much right now." He sounded relieved.

There was the longest silence, slightly awkward but surprisingly comforting.

"Are you still there?" I asked, eventually. He didn't reply, but I could hear his breathing. "Lex?"

For the first time I could sense vulnerability in him. I wasn't even sure that someone like him was capable of being insecure. He had always had things together. As a boy he was buzzing, always active and energised. I'd followed him on social media for the past few years and his life was like something out of 'Riverdale', minus the drama.

"I'm here." He laughed. As the sound echoed down the phone, I shook off my concern, but imagined a slight mocking tone to his humour.

"Ha, okay," I replied nervously.

"Anyway, I better go," he replied quickly. "I've got to be somewhere."

Nerves shook through my body and redness flushed to my cheeks.

"I'm glad you answered," he added softly. "Speak later?"

"Okay," I replied and hung up quickly.

ALEXANDER

"You have grown up into such a strong young man," Mrs Herbert said, pulling me into an intense hug as I entered the house. "Your mum has been telling me all about how amazing and helpful you are to her."

"Yeah?" I smiled back at her, a little surprised that Mum had even noticed. "I try to help out where I can, I guess."

"Leave him alone, Sarah."

Michael Herbert came toward us, grinning, with two beers in hand and the other hand beckoning me towards him.

"You still into sports, Alex?"

"Of course!" I followed him into the house, smiling at Sarah as I passed.

"Good!" He took a quick glance back at me. "Too young for a beer?"

"Uhm," I mumbled, unsure how to reply.

"Here." He passed me one he had clearly already intended for me. "It's nice to have another man in this house! How's your dad? Still golfing?"

"Yeah, he's good. Always golfing."

"I must arrange something with him soon." His eyes darted back to his wife as he spoke; clearly the Herbert family took Mum's side in the divorce.

"Yeah, he'd like that," I replied, trying to ease the newly found tension between the couple.

"Do you have a job?" Michael continued, staring straight at

me, clearly un-phased by how intense he was. Michael Herbert was a kind man; his stomach was beginning to poke forward and his hair balding. Before we moved away he was extremely well-kept and motivated. His business was booming and his life seemed almost perfect. My parents would often argue about how they should be more like the Herberts… or at least how Dad should be more like Michael. Yet now it was clear the years of hard work were taking a toll on him.

"I do odd bits for family friends, but nothing currently."

"Come visit me at work, I'll hook you up with a few construction jobs if you want," Michael added eagerly.

"Michael," Sarah snapped from the doorway. "You can't ask him things like that before speaking to Anna."

"The boy is seventeen," he blurted, spitting beer as he spoke. "I was working at seventeen. I'm sure he can decide for himself."

There was something weirdly comforting in them arguing over me. There was always arguing before my parents divorced, but it was never about me.

"I've got your back, lad," Michael added with a nudge to my shoulder.

"Romola. Dinner!" Sarah called a few minutes later. "Michael, can you help her please?"

"One minute, the game is just starting."

"You can catch the end afterwards!" she yelled back. "We are eating, NOW!"

It was surreal being in the middle of their argument, almost as though I had never left.

"We better go, kid."

The dinning room was set for four.

"Can I help you with anything, Sarah?"

"If you could grab some glasses, I'm almost ready. I hope you still like lasagne."

Mrs Herbert's lasagne was always the most incredible, loaded with cheese and the best tomato sauce.

"Yes!" I laughed. "Always."

She smiled for the first time since I'd been back.

"Good."

Her jaw dropped when she saw me sat at her dining room table. Michael carried her into the room, clearly un-phased by the fact that his daughter was only wearing a t-shirt and her legs and underwear were on full display to the entire room.

"Michael, quickly," Sarah snapped, clearly making the same realisation that I had. He hesitated, confused by his wife's remark. "Put her down. Alex is here."

I couldn't help but laugh.

"MUM!" Romola screamed, clearly more embarrassed by her mother's acknowledgement than being exposed.

"Alex doesn't seem to mind," Michael added, putting Romola onto a chair and sniggering to himself.

"DAD!" she shouted, her cheeks flooding with heat. As her eyes darted between her parents and me, I could feel my own face flush.

"Why are you here?" She scowled at me bitterly. "You said you were busy tonight."

I confess it was fun to watch her fight me, jealousy ringing in her voice.

"I am." I laughed, unaware of her parents. "Your parents invited me over for dinner."

"You could've said!"

"Where would be the fun in that?" I replied, but I could tell that she wasn't happy.

We stared at each other. I couldn't contain myself, I was beaming and she eventually joined me, until we were smirking like two kids concealing a secret. Sarah leant in to pass the garlic bread across the table. A look shot between Romola's parents as they acknowledged our squabble with each other, but we ignored it.

"Are you going to go to university, Alexander?" Mrs Herbert asked as she passed me the salad.

"MUM, that's so intense."

Sarah looked confused.

"Is it?"

"Ha-ha, no, it's cool," I replied, smiling at Romola. "I'm not really sure. I'd quite like to travel, or take a year out." I paused. "I'm also considering the army."

"You are?" Mrs Herbert replied, placing her fork down as she leant in for a deeper conversation. "Does Anna know this?"

I sat up straight.

"Uhm, no," I said clearing my throat, before cramming my mouth with another fork of lasagne to avoid the conversation.

"That's a big decision to make alone, Alexander," she continued. I was confused by her concern. "What do you think, Michael?"

As I sat at the familiar table, with familiar faces I wondered for a moment if I had dreamt the preceding years. I imagined how life might've been, had I remained here.

"I think it's his choice, Sarah, the boy is seventeen," Michael answered, piling more garlic bread onto his plate and waving his hand towards me.

Mrs Herbert scowled at her husband.

"I mean, you will think it through, right?" he added, to ease his wife's fury.

"Sure." I smiled "It's all just a thought."

My eyes darted to Romola who was desperately trying not to laugh. Her curly hair had fallen across her cheeks as she cowered forward to conceal herself. She was enjoying watching me squirm under the pressure of her parents.

"What about you Rome?" I added sheepishly

"Um." She darted a fierce look towards me.

"Romola's going to study business," Mrs Herbert interrupted. "It'll be good for when she takes over the business."

My eyes widened. Neither Romola nor her father looked at each other.

"Oh wow, really? No sixth form either?" I asked, confused.

"It's undecided," Michael added, shooting a smile towards his daughter. She relaxed her shoulders and leant in for another bite.

"Michael, you know we need her help for a while," Sarah continued.

"Yes, Sarah!" he added. "I know."

Romola looked at me a little hurt, but smiled gently.

"You finished eating?" she asked, watching me watch her.

I nodded.

"Don't forget the game, Alex," Michael mumbled through a mouthful of food. He was clearly not going to miss a chance for some lad time.

"I won't!" I replied "Fifteen minutes?"

He pointed his beer towards me in a nod.

"Can you carry me?" Romola was looking at me.

"Yeah, I can." I smiled. "Thank you for dinner, Sarah."

"You're welcome." She nodded before returning to scowl at

her husband.

Carrying her into her room, we quickly became aware of our proximity and the false confidence created in the dining room. One of my hands locked under her bare legs as I pulled her closer.

"Sorry that was so intense," she whispered, the words barely leaving her mouth.

"It's strange," I started to say, but I couldn't find the words to finish.

"Strange being here?" she added for me.

"Yeah. I mean your hallway is a time-line of our past."

We hovered a while staring at everything around us.

"It's like nothing has changed."

"And yet, everything has changed.," she finished, moving her gaze to mine and holding it there.

For the first time, I felt something.

ROMOLA

I had experienced two kisses in my life so far. The first was in year eight, when I was the subject of a school dare and got kissed in the playground by Nick Lewis. I have chosen to wipe that one clear from my mind because it was the worst, rushed kiss and felt strange. It ended in tears as I ran into the girls' locker room, sobbing that 'my first kiss had been stolen'.

The second kiss was last summer when I was dating Aden. The relationship lasted five weeks and was over the night we kissed. Having spent the majority of our relationship messaging, I can hardly say it was anything serious. We had a few real dates where I clenched my stomach and braved visiting the cinema with him, or going for a meal. It was the third date we moved to hand holding and the fifth date we kissed. It wasn't particularly the kiss that was bad, but everything that followed.

Aden's parents had gone away for the weekend and so I'd agreed to a movie night at his house. We ordered take-out and crashed on the sofa to watch Netflix. There is something that becomes quickly apparent when you first start dating, and that is that you know nothing about dating until you start.

We finished the pizza; I ate as much as I could stomach, but I was too anxious to eat much. The room rang silent. I stared at the TV confused, waiting for him to flick to Netflix so we could chill. But he just sat, watching me for a while. There is a way of knowing when you are about to be kissed and it's all in the eyes. As they assess the situation, they will always look for eye contact before they make their move. They lock, staring deep into your pupils for a moment – so far that you fear they can see into your soul. This is when your stomach either flips or doesn't; this is the moment you know you are lost. When you are new to being kissed, it is easy to miss these signs, so I just smiled and stared intently back. My expression was encouragement enough for him to lean in and fully plant his slippery mouth against mine. The kiss was sweet and gentle. It was the first kiss I had imagined years ago, although it tasted slightly salty after the pizza. It was sweet and perfect, but it didn't last long as Aden quickly moved onto something more. Pushing me back against the sofa, he pulled his body onto mine and found his way into my underwear. His fingers moving swiftly against my body, I was momentarily paralysed. I was a teenager and other people in my year were doing this, so I allowed it for a few moments whilst I tried to make sense of what was happening. For a brief moment I was lost in his desire, but I knew I didn't want it; I did not consent. I didn't even really like Aden and it hurt a little. I shot up fiercely, pushing him away. Pulling my knickers as high as they could go, desperate to cover myself, I grabbed my things and sprinted out of the house, tears finding their way down my cheeks. That was the last time I had been kissed and the first time I had found myself in an unknown world. It was the last time I spoke to Aden, or even thought of another guy, until Lex.

"You've changed too," Lex said, laughing a little, his voice sounding nervous. "You used to hide away behind books and writing. Now you're going to Business School, what's that about?"

He opened my bedroom door and placed me gently against my bed. Lex was clearly not going to kiss me. As soon as he put me down, he moved towards the window, almost as far away as he could from where I was. He was tense, like the nervousness I had sensed was pacing up and down his body. I could feel my own stomach beginning to waver.

"That's not what I want," I replied, cowering my head low and pulling a cushion to my stomach.

"Then why?" he asked, abruptly. He was flicking through the piles of books dotted around my room.

"I don't know. My mum asked me to do it for a few years, to help them get moving and then I'll go to university later. My dad isn't happy about it, but I think he's just disappointed in himself."

Lex turned to look at me now.

"You're so strong, Rome," he stated, as though it were a fact.

I couldn't help but snigger aloud; if only he'd known what was erupting in my stomach.

"Do you still write?" he asked a few minutes later, still pacing my room and flicking through pages pinned to my wall.

"All the time."

"Can I read some?" he asked, turning to me eagerly.

"No way." I could feel my face reddening as I pictured him reading my words. "They're too… personal."

He was smiling now, almost as though he was ignited by my bashfulness.

"Okay, Rome, so what did you invite me in here to do?"

My room was dark, lit only by two small lamps at either end of the room. Alex had always had his hair in the same close shave, but it was grown out a little now. The tight curls at the top of his head faded down into a smooth shadow above his neckline, perfectly framing his jaw. His ebony skin was so dark in the dim light of my room; I couldn't see him clearly but could trace his figure with my eyes. He was so different now, his body strong and shaped, and yet so familiar.

"I just thought we could hang out," I managed to peel from my lips, but my heart had begun to dance with my stomach, teasing each other. It sounded ridiculous to say aloud.

He moved towards me and I felt certain he was going to kiss me now.

"Let's hang out then." He laughed and moved so quickly his entire body leaped onto the bed next to me. But he just lay there, staring up at the ceiling. "So much has changed," he repeated, quietly and to himself.

I lay back against my pillow, resolved to the fact that I was not going to be kissed, but certain that I wanted him to more than anything in the world. I watched him thinking and wanted to know everything about him. He felt like home to me, and yet we had lived entirely separate lives.

"Are you happy?" I asked, without even realising I had.

He didn't reply but turned onto his side and nodded; I didn't believe him.

"Are you?" he asked.

I nodded.

"But I am now," he said finally.

"Me too."

We barely spoke for the next few minutes. Occasionally one of us would start talking, but it quickly ended and we just lay there. There was a conversation in our silence.

My dad eventually called him in for the game and our peace was disturbed. I didn't bother to pull myself up; I just let him start to leave. My body was too fragile, emotions battling against each other inside.

"Hey, Rome." He turned around to look at me as he reached

the door.

"Yeah."

"I wanted to kiss you, but I don't know if it's okay yet."

I couldn't reply. He left and I spent the next few minutes temporarily paralysed by anxiety, listening to Lex and my dad laughing together in my living room.

ALEXANDER

I decided to drive into the city. I hadn't seen Dad since we'd moved. He was always the easiest person to be around when the last thing you wanted to do was to think. The roads were quiet this early. I hadn't managed to sleep much last night, so decided to make an early start. The thought of kissing Romola played over in my mind, with different scenarios each time. I had no idea why I said it; wrapped up in the moment it was exactly what I wanted. Saying it aloud to her over-complicated everything. We were too interwoven. If I screwed this up it would pull apart our family and I'd lose much more than a girl. She wasn't just any girl. I kept picturing her lying next to me, her cute oversized t-shirts failing to cover her legs. Anyone would've been attracted to her, especially knowing she wanted it too. But I wasn't anyone and she wasn't anyone. Besides, I was dating Alice, and I wasn't ready for that to end.

"You up for golfing?" Dad asked the moment I arrived at his.

He lived in a modern block of flats in the centre of the city, built in an old warehouse. The apartment was minimally designed and every corner screamed independence. Two tall house plants graced the corners of the apartment, cared for weekly by his cleaner. It was strange to think that he even had a cleaner. When he lived with us, he was always cleaning the house. It was his way of avoiding other things and still getting away with 'doing' enough. It had been almost a year since he left Mum the house. Nothing had really changed to his new space since then, but something was different.

"Uh, yeah," I replied, chucking my bag onto the sofa. "You got some coffee first?"

Dad grinned; he was always proud of his espresso machine and ability to make the best flat white. I wasn't a big fan of coffee before he bought it, but he spent endless weekends perfecting his barista art that it eventually became impossible to avoid.

"I've got a new one!" He looked like a child at Christmas.

He had an ease about him that reminded me of myself, or at least the version of myself that found life easy. His smile spread across his face, lifting gently higher at one side.

"A new machine?" I asked, shocked.

"Nope. A new combination."

I laughed at him, following him into his kitchen space and sitting on a bar stool as he worked on the coffee.

"Okay, hear me out," he began, with his back to me, clearly mixing together syrups.

The divorce had been great for him. I didn't begrudge him for it either; it wasn't like he'd chosen not to take me on. Honestly, I was much more myself and could relax here; part of me wished I had chosen to live here.

"This one is hazelnut, salted caramel with a hint of mint." He laughed, passing me a perfectly made latte.

"Wow, Dad, you have truly outdone yourself here," I replied sarcastically.

"Don't knock it 'til you've tried," he said, turning back to make one for himself. I was a little reluctant to drink the potion in front of me, but was pleasantly surprised by the sweet nutty coffee.

"Okay, I take it back." I laughed, putting the drink down for a minute to fully appreciate the kick. "You might have a talent here."

"How's your mum?" he asked almost immediately and I wondered how he'd managed to last this long.

"Yeah, she's okay."

He was reading me. His face always looked slightly lost when he tried to work things out. I knew it was hopeless for him, there was nothing to understand in my face; I had already perfected blankness.

"Alex. I've started dating again," he eventually spoke, his words crisp and deep, crackling slightly as he cleared his throat.

"Okay," I replied without delay, unsure how to respond. My parents' divorce wasn't easy, but then nothing seemed easy any more. The worst part about it for me was the separation; selfishly I didn't even care if they were still together. And yet, giving a hearty approval at my dad's newfound pastime wasn't appropriate, especially when Mum wasn't okay.

"She'd like to meet you," Dad continued, sipping nervously at his coffee."

"So you're not 'dating' then," I replied. "You're seeing someone."

My voice was bitter; I was clearly more affected than I'd let myself believe.

"For the past two months. It's still really early days, but I do like her a lot."

In this moment I felt like I was the adult. The truth was that I had never spoken to Dad about things like this, even my own. We never spoke about anything important to me.

"Oh, okay." I tried to sound slightly more enthusiastic, but even with my grumbling he jumped at the slight acceptance.

"Okay, great, kid. I'll plan something for next weekend?"

I nodded. If I had found some way to avoid it, we'd only end up back here in a week; it was un-avoidable.

The golf pitch was swarming on a Saturday morning. Being with Dad at the club was like being the son of a celebrity. He had an energy that made everyone seem welcome and wanted.

"Zane." A tall grey-haired man gestured to my dad as we arrived at the club. "You up for a round?"

"Not today, mate, I'm with Alex today. My son."

The amount of times I had been golfing with him, he still felt the need to introduce me as his son. Even being this close to the city, we were almost always the only black people at the club. It could've been this that made us stand out initially, but dad definitely left his mark. He was never one to acknowledge things like that, he barely ever felt uncomfortable. It was something I had adopted and made socialising easy. I wondered sometimes if he was also less certain underneath it all, like I was. That was a topic we would never discuss together.

"You still with Elle?" Dad asked as I took my turn. He was great at talking just as I was about to hit.

"Ha-ha, typical Dad." I laughed as I missed. "Nah, not any more."

"Nice try," he mocked. "Anyone new to the scene?"

I thought of Alice and Romola, wondering if this might be an opportunity to talk.

"Uh, not really."

I felt uneasy, so I avoided the subject.

"Still early days," he continued. "Besides, I know you don't have to worry about things; you've always been bright, but it's worth studying now. Have you decided on a university? You could definitely get into Cambridge with your grades, son. I had a great time there, as you know."

There were times like this, playing golf and talking about the 'golden triangle' schools that I couldn't feel more different to my father.

"Yeah, I just don't know. I still have a year."

I almost told him about taking time away from studying but I knew it wouldn't go well. He would talk about my privilege and how hard he had worked for the opportunities he had. So I bit my lip and smiled.

"You worried I'm gonna win this game." I laughed.

"In your dreams!" He laughed, moving back onto banter topics. The best thing about Dad was that he was far too busy to worry.

ROMOLA

Town was full, locals swarming the shops and cafes like they did every Saturday. It was strange being in the car, watching the world move fast around me. I was not used to being inactive, but could appreciate being in the car was better than my room. I watched mothers rushing around, pulling their young children faster than their feet could manage, as they rushed about to do errands. There was a particular corner of town that was always filled with youths, who had little to do besides hang around on a bench. The cafes were always bustling, as cafe culture became the sole form of social interaction. I was a frequent visitor to all the local cafes. Cally and I made it our purpose to visit them all as often as each other – so long as they had good cake. We had carefully rated them into order of cake, but my favourite was "Beanies". I had worked there for almost two years every Saturday and it had become a second home to me. It was a 'family run' business and I was able to be myself when I worked there. It wasn't directly in town, but closer to Crow Hill and operated more as a walking cafe. Our regulars were usually sixty-plus or mum-and-toddler groups.

"It's nice to get away," I said to Mum as we drove out of town, towards the hill. "I just can't wait to be able to walk up Crow Hill like we normally do."

"Soon!" Mum replied with a smile.

We hadn't spent a lot of time together in the past few years. I almost always made myself scarce around my parents. Every

Saturday before work Mum and I would race up the hill, it was something we did before I started at "Beanies".

"Romola," Jan called as Mum wheeled me into the cafe. "So great to see you. How are you?"

Jan looked like an ex-punk rocker, her hair always tied into two long plaits that hung around her waist. She was in her late fifties but looked not a year over forty, and far too beautiful to spend her days in a cafe in the middle of no-where. "Beanies" was Jan's baby. She ran the cafe with her husband and employed her two nephews – both of whom were older than me, but had become like brothers to me.

"Look who is here," she called towards the kitchen. Liam was the eldest; he was twenty-eight and was the biggest geek you could meet. His hair was a mousey brown halo of wavy curls; the result of being too lazy to get a haircut. Jan always made him tie it back but parts of it always fell to his neck neglectfully. The younger brother was Sam, he was twenty-five and completely gorgeous.

"Oiy oiy," Sam called, storming into the kitchen with his arms wide. He was perfect and yet to me he was just Sam.

"What did you do to yourself, Romy?" he laughed. "Anything to get out of a bit of work, hey!"

"Hardly." I laughed. "I miss this place!"

"We miss you too," Jan replied.

"Yeah, we miss you doing all the work so we can sit back and sip coffee," Sam teased.

Liam followed through a few minutes later, carrying his laptop and a coffee. He was the PR and marketing genius for the cafe and had successfully made it a walkers' and cyclists' hot spot.

"What's up, Romola?" He smiled when he saw me. "How are you?"

"I mean, I've been better." I laughed.

As fun as Sam was, Liam was the one I could talk to the most. In fact, he was constantly checking in over the past few weeks.

"I've got something to tell you." He couldn't stop grinning.

"YOU DIDN'T." I laughed, knowing exactly what he was going to say.

"Yes, I'm getting married to Jenny."

Sam rolled his eyes and moved back to the counter where he could sneak a croissant whilst we were talking.

"We're thinking next summer, so get your feet moving. I have a lousy best man so I'll need your help." He laughed, nodding towards Sam and fully disclosing his secret croissant.

"There's nothing lousy about me."

Jan shook her head at them both, pulling a seat up for mum and making us drinks.

It was great to be there and for a moment I forgot about everything else, caught up in the plans for the future.

"So, Romola, is it nice to get out of the house?" Mum asked. She was the only person to still call me Romola all the time and I liked that.

"It's so great, thank you, Mum." It was different being out with her; it was normal. I didn't have the added complications that came with Lex.

"I need to talk to you about something," she began but was quickly disrupted by the sound of plates crashing in the kitchen. We both looked over to see Sam clearing up a broken bowl of porridge.

"Sure, tell me anything," I replied, happily enjoying the normality of life.

"Oh, um," she said, half distracted by Sam and half taking note of my enthusiasm. "Well, as you know, things aren't great at home; with Michael and myself."

She spoke as though this should've been a revelation to me. I watched her intently as she spoke, waiting on each word with desperation. I wondered if this were the moment she would tell me that my life was to separate. I looked around at the cafe. It was mostly quiet but for a few customers dotted around. This was a place that was mine and was full of such joy. The memories that filled these walls were positive; I couldn't help but feel that this was going to ruin them all. She looked bright, like a weight was pulling away from her with every word. For a moment I felt her release, watching my mother come alive in front of me. I could see the future; I could see her happiness coming back to her. This feeling was fleeting and I trod it down with all the anger that I had hidden away. With each moving muscle that spread a deeper smile across her face, I felt furious at the selfishness of her joy. I wanted to scream, but I was here, in my safe space. I wondered then if that was why she chose it.

"Yeah, I do," I spat through gritted teeth, avoiding her eyes in hope that my anger was clear.

"It's okay," she replied sweetly, like she knew what I was thinking. That was the worst thing about mothers, they always knew. I felt like a three-year-old again, quickly comforted by the warm words of my mum. "We have decided to give it another go."

I felt confused. It wasn't what I thought she would say but something about the words "another go" made me feel like things had ended for them.

"We're going to have marriage counselling and really make things work this time. For all three of us."

I kept thinking about what Lex had said about his parents staying together for him; was this what she meant? Did I want that?

"Wow. When?"

"Well, we've decided to start the counselling when you go back to school. Things are very busy now."

I nodded at her and smiled a little.

ALEXANDER

I had been joining Dad at the golf course most weekends, for the majority of my life. It was a dream of his that I would take to the sport and would want to play professionally. I often wondered if this was where things took a sour turn for my parents' marriage. Dad was always away; if not at the local golf club, he would be on a golfing retreat with friends. Mum went occasionally, she had even had an interest in it when they met, but that soon fizzled when she realised she would come second to golf in his life. It was okay until I decided not to share the same keen interest. For a while I tried to keep it up, attending all the coaching he bought me or joining him on weekends. Eventually I told him I didn't want to do it forever and almost immediately the rows began at home. They weren't good before, so even if I had nudged them towards divorce, it was inevitable. The thing I lost most from it all was our relationship. Dad and I barely hung out for my early teenage years and only really re-connected when they eventually divorced. It was like any time we spent together was part of a schedule, so I couldn't be avoided. Golf became his thing; he would occasionally invite me, but that was rare.

"What do you want to eat, kid?" he asked as we arrived back at his that night. We had been at the club all day.

"Can we order in?" I asked, already knowing the answer. Dad hated cooking.

"Totally. Pizza?"

I nodded.

Dad looked over at the buzzing phone next to me.

"You gonna answer that?" he said through a mouthful of pizza.

"Nah, I'll catch them later."

Alice was calling. She had called a couple of times in the day, but I hated phone conversations.

Being at Dad's flat was the break I needed from everything. It wasn't like home, where I didn't want to burden Mum with my presence. Here I could be whoever I wanted to be and there would be no judgment. Dad passed me a second beer and I began devouring another slice of pizza. The more I thought about it, he was a crap father. There was no real conversation about life or what was happening to me. Occasionally I saw him look at me with a small look of concern but he brushed it off. Yet, despite his shitty parenting, he was exactly what I needed right now. A space to go and just do nothing.

We stayed up until the early morning, stuffing our faces, gaming and watching 'Brooklyn 99' on Netflix.

It was late morning when I finally woke – slightly confused by the messy living room around me; I had fallen asleep on the sofa. At home there was never mess, not even after a night in front of the TV. Mum always wanted things clean and ready for the next day; she was always doing something the following morning that meant she wanted a clear space. Sundays were church mornings, followed by entertaining friends. The last time I had slept until noon was pre-divorce.

"S'up kid," Dad called from the kitchen. He was already showered and making coffee. "Did you sleep well?"

"Uh, yeah," I replied, still a little disorientated.

"Great. Coffee?" he asked, already pouring me a cup.

"Thanks."

"So I was thinking," he began, his voice a little deep. "We could do something before you go home today?"

The thought of going home made my stomach turn slightly and I regretted drinking coffee straight away.

"Yeah, what like?"

I was hoping he'd suggest rock climbing. It was what we did together post-golf and I actually loved climbing. It was incredible doing something that was controlled by physical strength. I felt indestructible when I climbed.

"I was thinking you could meet Rachel," he added, staring directly at me so it was almost impossible to say no. He was always good at confrontation. Throughout my parents' marriage, he would avoid anything Mum said until an argument broke out and then he would straighten up and was so alert it was almost impossible to remember your own thoughts. It was his lawyer mannerisms – always prepared to defend. Eventually Mum and I gave up even attempting to argue.

"Uh, okay," I replied, confused. "So you don't want me to come for dinner?"

"Oh no, definitely do that too. I just thought it might be good to briefly meet today."

Either he had changed, or this was Rachel's thought.

"I'll go shower."

I was reminded what life was like with Dad: unpredictable. It was what made it super fun, but also made for the worst husband or parent when he never came home on time or would cancel plans at the last minute. We made exceptions for his work; being a corporate lawyer meant that he was often caught at work, but eventually it became much more. I felt the same disappointment flush over me now, as I would waiting for him to come to a football match or take me to the cinema.

Rachel's house was on the other side of the city, so we met in town. It was different being here now; it was no longer home.

"Do you prefer Alex or Alexander?" was the first thing Rachel asked.

She was younger than Dad, in her early thirties. Her blonde hair was cut bluntly at her shoulders and swayed gently as she spoke with a bouncy energy. Dressed immaculately in a smart skirt and jacket, she looked like someone from a US TV series. I recognised her from his office parties; we would all attend them before the divorce.

"Alex is cool," I replied. I wasn't expecting to, but I felt angry. It was weird because she seemed so together... like Mum never was... like I wasn't. Part of me couldn't help feeling that we had been traded in for a more groomed version.

She continued chatting at me for a while. I politely replied, but gave very little away. It was quickly clear that there was no room for me here; there was no opportunity to live with Dad. My defences shot up quicker than expected and I couldn't relax. This was not my life.

I stayed for an hour, before making an excuse that I had to get home early.

The roads were quiet and when I arrived back home I felt a strange relief to see Mum waiting at the door. She looked tired, wearing her yoga trousers and a hoodie. There was nothing groomed about her, but the look of excitement when she saw me walk towards her reminded me why I had chosen to live with her. Despite the chaos of her life, she was real.

ROMOLA

I hadn't spoken to Lex since the dinner at our house. I was glad; I needed things to be normal for a while. My stomach had managed to calm itself and my anxiety was dormant for a few days. My parents were clearly trying out a new '*Let's be friends*' method and it was awkward to be around. It wasn't like they were being normal and simply being kinder to each other. They had devised a plan to spend time together and do activities. It was great, if not a little amusing to see them trying, but it felt forced. Dad wasn't watching his sport with a beer in front of the TV any more and Mum wasn't out with her friends all the time. They were just there, always around each other, hardly doing anything. I hoped it was just teething problems to a great solution but I knew it was destined for failure.

"Can you rescue me?" Lex asked on the phone the following Thursday evening. Neither of us mentioned what he had said to me on Friday.

"Maybe. It depends if it would benefit me," I said teasingly.

For the first time I felt worried about what I was saying. It was different now I knew he felt similar to me, that it wasn't just another one of my silly infatuations. At least I thought he felt similar to me, but the delayed conversation this week sent me into a nagging confusion. The thought that this could be *something* terrified me. It occurred to me that I didn't know how to sound cool or flirty. I didn't really know how to speak to Lex as anything other than the dorky girl from his childhood.

He was laughing on the phone, a sweet, gentle confirmation of my terrible attempt to be charming.

"Well, I have a dinner with Dad and his new girlfriend and I can't bare going alone."

"He has a new girlfriend? How are you about that?"

"It's fine," he replied, but it was clear that it wasn't okay.

"Will you come?"

"Yeah, totally."

The nerves rushed back to my stomach like the blood was pushing pins and needles into my feet. It was as though I had completely forgotten the sensation, until it flooded back to its familiar space. I felt safe with Lex; he was familiar and kind. There was no reason to feel un-easy, and yet there was something in my gut that wouldn't let me rest.

Typically, it takes me hours to decide what to wear, I will even find some way to embellish the school uniform. That Thursday I couldn't think all day. There was nothing important about what I would wear, because there was nothing more important than the event itself. The last words Lex had said to me the night of the dinner played over in my head like a jukebox on repeat. I had casually accepted the invitation to dinner without considering the fact that something could happen.

"What's she like?" I asked Lex as he climbed into the car.

He looked smart, in a crisp white shirt and dark denim jeans. I could feel my insides begin to dance.

"She's very well maintained," he replied as though he was describing his dad's latest coffee machine. For a moment I wasn't sure he was serious, but there was something about his manner that made me sure this wasn't an attribute he wanted her to have.

I scanned down at my black lace dress. I hadn't worn a dress in years but it was much easier than attempting to wear anything else. I felt childish, like my thirteen-year-old self who had bought the dress in H&M. My cheeks began to heat with embarrassment.

"It's good," he continued, unaware of my momentary stress. "Dad's always wanted someone like that. They fit together well, for work purposes."

It was the first time I had heard Lex speak with resentment towards his father. In fact, he never spoke badly of either of his parents. Sometimes I wondered if he felt indebted to them for something; he was always rushing around to please them.

"That's good then; that they're suited to each other, I mean."

He looked at me as I replied and it was as though he had forgotten who I was. It was as though I was a hitchhiker and he was unsure why I was commenting on his personal life. For this brief moment I also couldn't recognise Lex; everything about him looked blank and unfamiliar. I couldn't help wondering if there was darkness to him, beneath the banter. We sat in silence the rest of the way. As the motorway channeled into the city and buildings grew taller around us we both began to relax. I felt nervous around Lex a lot of the time, even the thought of him made my bones tense, but this was different. There was a coldness about him that froze us both into confusion. It was a relief to see his shoulders drop and a small smile curl up to his eyes.

"Thank you for coming with me," he added, before nudging me on the shoulder with a slight nervousness, as though he knew I had seen him. Really seen him.

ALEXANDER

I had made a mistake bringing her into the city. It was much more difficult to be Lex here, I had only ever been Alex. I had only ever been the worst version of myself. I could feel it sweeping over me like lead filling into my blood. I was thankful for the straight road as my feet stuck to the accelerator. I had never felt nervous before. I was the type of person who could switch off or change character whenever a weakness presented itself. Funerals were always the worst because I found it almost impossible to cry. Driving into the city with her I felt my guard slip and couldn't pull up a defence. Nothing functioned; nothing would move or change. I wasn't afraid. I didn't know what to feel, I didn't know what I should've felt. So I froze.

Walking up to Dad's building, I watched her carefully for signs of concern but she remained composed. Her hair was pulled back into a low bun, it was the first time I had ever seen her like this. She was wearing makeup and dressed up in a short black dress. She always looked cute in her oversized t-shirt and messy hair that she frantically tried to flatten every time I walked in. This was different; she had really dressed up for this and looked incredible. I knew she could feel me watching her, but there was something about her tonight that made it impossible to look away.

"Romola. WELCOME!" Dad bellowed as I wheeled her in through the door. "How are you? Alexander told me about your accident. It can't be long now until you're up and about?"

"Hey! Hopefully not," she replied. "I should be getting checked next week."

"Excellent," he added.

There was no sign of Rachel but the entire place echoed her vision. I could see it now and knew it was here last week. It was the small things, like the increasing number of living plants dotted around; Dad would never be able to keep a plant alive on his own.

"This looks like a great place!" Romola gestured to Dad. "Do you play?" She was pointing at a piano in the corner of the room. It hadn't been there last week.

"Rachel does and I'm attempting to learn," he replied enthusiastically.

I could feel anger pumping into my wrists as I clenched my fist tight to diffuse the fury. During my parents' divorce I hadn't felt anything, yet now I could feel it all rushing in like a burst dam. It was as though everything was different. Here, everything was new and nothing about it made sense.

"Does she live here?" I scoffed, kissing my teeth as I scanned the room. He didn't see, or chose not to. There was a delay to his response that made me certain he had.

"Occasionally," he finally replied.

I just nodded.

"Romola, Hello!" Rachel said, rushing through the door with a bag of shopping from Wholefoods. "I've heard a lot about you. Alexander, how are you doing?"

"I'm good," I snubbed, turning away and planting myself on the sofa next to Romola.

"Hello," she replied to Rachel, frowning at me and nudging me slightly. "All good things, I hope?"

"Yes, all good. Except for your most recent accident. That

must've been terrible."

"It was, but it's okay now and Lex has kept me entertained."

I looked up at her. She was smiling sweetly at me, clearly attempting to pull me out of my newly discovered grump.

"More like tormenting you." I sniggered, jolting up a little.

"Trying to, but he's really lost his touch," she teased.

Rachel seemed content with the conversation and nodded towards the kitchen where she retreated.

"She seems nice," Romola continued when we were left alone.

I shrugged.

"She's okay."

There was a short silence that quickly closed our distance. I could hear her breath deepen. She was nervous.

"You look incredible," I mumbled slightly as I turned towards her. The words seemed to be of little comfort as heat flushed to her face. Her body tensed inwards as she clenched her arms across her chest.

"Thank you," she whispered, barely loud enough to hear. I leant across slightly so that I could reach her hand, winding my fingers between hers as she sighed outwards.

"Sorry I'm being such a dick."

But she didn't reply. We just sat there for a while lost in the heated entwinement of our fingers.

Rachel was a great cook. I was ready to let it send me over the top; something inside me was desperate to cause a reaction. I could feel this new fury urging me to shout and tip the table over. Yet I held back, not for my dad or Rachel. It wasn't even for Romola. It was for that small fragment of myself that I clung to somewhere inside, the small part of me that didn't want to fuck everything up.

"Thank you for dinner," I mouthed lightly at Rachel afterwards. Her face lit up, like she had just received a top grade on a school paper. For a moment I felt a little guilt at my hatred for her; she was desperately trying to impress me. In fact, none of this was her fault, she was just a by-stander that held the key to my shielded pain. I didn't begrudge her for my mother, but myself. With Rachel, my dad was content in a life separate to mine. A life he had always been content with. The bastard didn't give a fuck about me and this new life made that clear.

"Fuck, Rome, can we get out of here?" I whispered after the dessert.

"Uh, yeah. If you want."

I thought about running away to my bedroom with her, far enough to be separate to Dad and Rachel but still polite enough to stay longer. But there was something about being in my bedroom with Romola that made me feel un-easy. Or perhaps I didn't trust myself to stay distant with her. I was, after all, still with Alice; *wasn't I?*

"I should probably not stay too late, if that is all right?" Romola asked, nodding at me as she spoke. She had clearly witnessed my delay, and was rescuing me.

"Oh yeah, of course." I grinned. "Is it okay if we head back now, Dad?"

"Sure, kid. It was great to have you both here."

He smiled, unaware that I was already standing and poised ready to sprint.

"It was so great to meet you, Romola, and see you again, Alexander," Rachel added innocently.

"You too," we said, before leaving the flat as swiftly as possible.

ROMOLA

The lights fell and the roads darkened as we drove out of the city. I came alive at night; it was when my body was most calm and mind settled. I would often stay awake late, just to know the peace of the empty hours. There was nothing expected at night. It was always my happy place until the early morning would chime and the threat of the new day hung over me.

As we drove I could feel the warmth rise in the car again.

"Do you want to stop somewhere?" Lex asked. His words sliced through the silence, pulling me out of my thoughts.

"Uh, yeah sure," I replied, wondering if he wanted to talk about what was bothering him. I had always been the agony aunt of my friends. I was so confused by my friendship with Lex and I was desperate for him to clarify something, anything about what he was thinking.

"That was pretty awkward tonight?" He laughed, pulling into a viewpoint just off the country roads. We weren't far from home now.

"It was fine," I replied, cautiously. "I enjoyed myself."

His eyes showed a little relief as I spoke; I knew he was embarrassed by everything.

"Good. It wasn't exactly the best night to invite you to."

He was silent for a while. I watched him shift in his seat; his actions were strange, almost as though he was uncomfortable.

"Lex, are you okay?"

"Ha-ha, YEAH, I'm great." He laughed, without looking at

me.

"No, I mean, really okay?"

He stared out the front window, fighting for a reply.

"Fuck, I don't know." He sighed.

I waited for him to continue, but he didn't speak. It was as though he couldn't speak. He just stared.

"You can tell me, you know," I mumbled, nervously. It felt strange offering advice to him. For the past few weeks it was I who had been depending on him. In fact, he had always been the strength, the one to tease me or carry me. He was the one who had left and created a new life, his experiences trumped mine tenfold. Yet, in this moment, I was ignited and strong. I reached over to him, interlocking my fingers into his.

"Maybe one day," he replied eventually and I knew he meant it.

We stared a while at each other, lost in the darkness of the night and the outline of our faces. Our fingers began to dance in the darkness, locking and unlocking as they teased. It was platonic, the touch of reassurance. Until slowly I could feel his fingers drifting up my arm, moving in circles as they followed the curves upwards. My body began to tingle in response. We didn't move our eyes, it was as though they were fixed together, but it felt calm. I focused on his fingers tracing my shoulder and drifting around my neck as he pulled me closer to him. The space between us closed and our lips were pressed together, moving gradually within the embrace.

I could feel my eyes filling with heat. I was electric and powerful. For the first time anxiety had no place with me. It was unwelcome and didn't dare enter. For the first time it was me there, conscious and happy. I didn't want it to end but knew that if I continued it might never be anything more than sex. Part of me didn't mind that either. Lost in the feverish energy of lust, I wanted nothing but him. But I wasn't ready for it. Even though I knew that I wanted it to be with him. There was no judgment, just us.

I occasionally wonder what would've happened if that night had ended differently. If I had allowed my feverish lust to take over, and pulled myself closer to him. I imagined it for the enjoyment of picturing Lex close to me, giving him to me fully because we were united in each other's passion. That was the version I enjoyed most of all. I was powerful in that version.

The other version was where I imagined the ripples that followed a night like that. Had we committed ourselves to sex, the following days might've played out differently. And yet we didn't, and they still played out like a nightmare.

"Are you looking forward to going back?" Mum asked me the night before returning to school. She was eerily happy, like something had changed. She was even brushing her hair in the mornings – she had given that up when she gave birth to me. I couldn't help but wonder if I had been wrong and that my parents' new methods of marriage maintenance were working.

"Ecstatic." I grinned a false smile.

"You must be excited to see Cally?"

I just nodded.

I'd spent the last week alone, with my parents. Lex messaged me every day, but I couldn't reply. Eventually he gave up. Mum grew cautious as I blamed my vomiting on tiredness and loss of appetite on painkillers. When he stopped communicating the demon left again. Mum's mind settled and my fears of being a spinster merged into acceptance. Helped greatly by a binge-watch of the Bridget Jones Trilogy… until she lived happily ever after.

My phone buzzed loudly at dinner. I could feel two stern looks from my parents, as I disobeyed the no-phone-at-the-table rule. As soon as I'd checked the screen I regretted my disobedience.

Alexander Hayward sent you a message.

7.45 p.m.
AH: I'll see you tomorrow, Miss Herbert.

My face became pin art.
"Romola?" Mum coughed, annoyed at my phone. I slid it onto my lap and picked at my remaining dinner. But I had lost my appetite.

It felt like the first day of school again; another chance to start over. I repeated positive affirmations to drown out the fear.
"LOOK WHAT YOU MADE ME DO!" I screamed Taylor Swift's lyrics as I stumbled around my bedroom in my underwear. Reluctant to face the day ahead, I stared down at my uniform: navy blazer and turquoise tartan skirt. I was going to look like everyone else, but I was not going to be the same. You see, this is how high school works:

Cally – without consideration of the consequences will have vented at Alice Jennings.

Alice Jennings – all too eager for a new conquest will have consulted the B*tch Squad.

B*tch Squad – new victim named: ROMOLA HERBERT

Enter absolute hell.

This is how it played out for Polly Miles last year. She made out with Alice's latest crush at a party and a series of events later she no longer attended BWC.

I flung my socks at the wall, attempting to dance with my crutches, using the handles as a microphone. My phone buzzed:

7.45 a.m.
 AH: Wanna lift?

My stomach spun; maybe today wouldn't be so bad. I sat at my dressing table and began concealing my acne. I was no Kim K contour girl, but I wanted to at least try. Shading in different areas, I plastered makeup on my face, lengthening and curling my lashes.

8.05 a.m.
 RH: 8.30?

You are a strong, independent woman, I told myself as I put the phone down – I might pay for this later. I placed my hand on my stomach, but with Lex by my side today I could face anything.

As his car pulled up to the drive my stomach swam in circles, crashing against my ribs before diverting towards my gut. I scanned the neighbourhood for anyone to see this moment – a guy picking me up for school – but there was no one. Mum and dad had already left for work, so not even they could see this momentous moment in my life, although if they had been, they would've just seen Lex. He was *just* Lex, that annoying boy who teased me. Can I really feel like this?

"You ready?" He grinned at me, leaning through the passenger seat window.

"Coming," I called. As I spoke my mouth turned dry, the last gulp of liquid burning through my body until everything tingled and my legs burnt. I sat down in his car. It felt so different to that first trip to the seaside; I had been so confident then. My dry mouth could not speak. His teeth were so white against his skin, making his smile melt into my eyes. It was weird seeing him in our school uniform; he made the blazer look amazing; I made it look dorky. Next to him I felt like a preppy schoolgirl.

"It suits you," I croaked, pointing at the jacket.

"Ha-ha, thanks." He grinned. "I'm not used to uniform, my last school didn't have one."

Neither of us spoke. I leant over to put the radio on. Was he nervous too? I could sense him watching me through the corner of his eye. I began to sing a little as Ed Sheeran played; I always sang when I was nervous. Lex knew this! I stopped, embarrassed to have given myself away, but he started singing louder than I had been. I laughed at him as he foolishly sang different voices. I felt comfortable again, calm, so I joined in. We sang like idiots as we drove on. I hadn't noticed him move, I was singing too energetically. My hand burnt with heat all over, channeling ripples to my stomach, which moved up my body into my chest, into my mouth. I could not breathe. I looked down at the source of chaos and saw his beautiful long fingers locked around mine. I did not move. I just stared out of the window, breathless.

Teenagers began to fill the streets as we approached the high school. Lex removed his clasp from mine, to navigate through the smaller roads. Pulling the sun shield mirror down, I attempted to act normal, checking my face and collecting my things together. *I can do this*, I thought, staring into my eyes to avoid exploding.

"Shall I carry your bags in for you?" Lex asked once we'd parked. I looked over at his chilled face and wide grin; there was no way I could walk next to him. Damaged legs aside, I had no idea how I was going to stand; my stomach was on fire!

"NO!" I burst. "It's fine, our tutor groups are in different directions anyway. Thanks for the lift."

I grabbed my bag, flung it over my back and hobbled as fast as possible out of the car into school. I needed Cally.

I pushed the school doors so loud they slammed against the walls; everyone stared hard at me. Their faces were raised a little with small smirks on the edges of their lips. *Seriously, guys, this can't be that funny!* Halfway down the corridor I realised the students were still smiling – why were they grinning? Was it my crutches? A few people laughed but worse than that were the pitying glares I got from random students. As the lockers turned towards the B*tch corner I knew what was happening. I had been played. Cally was stood next to Alice's locker, chatting away to her. She stopped as I walked by and gave me a pity glance with a dash of regret; but I knew I couldn't forgive her for what was about to happen. I knew that whatever it was, she had gone too far. Lex came running around the corner, and as I turned to look at him I saw the same look on his face I'd seen on so many others. PITY. I felt fooled – that handholding; the lift – was it all just to cushion the blow of whatever had happened? I couldn't bare it; I didn't want their pity. I could handle whatever it was... *after all how bad could it really be?*

Those are the words you hope never enter your mind at times like this. They are the words that send waves to the devil's accomplice, to intensify whatever is awaiting you around the corner. I turned away from the crowded corridor, into the bathroom. It was there, right in front of me... my biggest secret... that even *I* didn't know. Plastered across the walls were all the secrets that were pulling my family apart. Hundreds of the same poster covered the floor.

Centred on the page were my parents, one image of Dad taken in his office, hands on head. The second was Mum, caught in an embrace with Mr Thompson. I couldn't move my legs; they were nailed to the floor. My back slid down against the bathroom door, blocking the nudges to come in. I could hear Cally sobbing on the other side of the door. I wasn't sure why she was crying; I felt nothing.

Minutes passed that felt like hours.

I stared at the same bathroom I'd cried in a few years previous, staring at the acne face in front of me. This was the same bathroom Cally and I hid in to skive class in year nine, claying our faces in make up and gossiping about boys as we stalked classmates on Instagram. Now all I could see was my life torn, soaking into the puddled floor and dewy walls. My parents' faces were fading into the dirt of the floor. All I could do was chuck myself at them, scooping the soggy sheets into my hands. I began collecting all the sheets of paper, stuffing them into the bottom of my backpack, every last sheet, attempting to protect my parents from a secret that was already revealed.

Paper in my hand, I sunk back down and didn't move.

"*Romy, this is going to be harder than we thought,*" I said to myself. "*You are a social outcast now.*"

"Romy," Cally called from the other side. "I'm sorry."

She was silent for a while; I almost thought she'd gone.

"Romy, I knew she was going to do something, I just didn't know this," she continued through sobs. My body froze as she spoke. "I was cross too, after the other day, and Alice said something was happening with Alexander, and now that they are dating... she said she would just give you a hint."

I couldn't speak; I had nothing to say to her.

"Romola, I'm so sorry."

She left.

ALEXANDER

I wish I could say that I had no idea what had happened, that I hadn't seen Romola head into the bathroom. I wish I could say that I went to comfort her; that I decided to be the kind of person that would go to someone in need. Someone that was more important to me than myself. I wish I wasn't about to make the worst decision I had ever made. This was the ultimate test of my humanity and I failed. Worse, I walked straight past the girls' bathroom and cowered. Perhaps if she had spoken, if it hadn't been utterly silent, her voice would've stirred something inside me and urged me to check in. But that wasn't for her to do and that didn't happen. I was a young boy again, afraid to be unliked.

ROMOLA

The harrowing school bell rang twice. I waited ten minutes before I knew the coast would be clear. I stood up and wiped the dried mascara from my cheek with a damp paper towel, scrubbing hard at the already red face. I scanned the toilets for any hidden posters, before heading out into the corridor. It was empty. Nothing was changed, it might all have been a dream but for the sickness in my chest. The corridor felt never-ending as I glided, unconscious, through the red locker room. The occasional face would catch the corner of my eye as I passed a classroom, filled with students unaware of my trauma. Their day would resume, their lives untouched. The joys of fitting in were that you never had to feel anything, no freedom, but no pain. That was me, before. I caught a glimpse of my locker, next to Cally's. We'd paid a student all our birthday money in year seven to swap lockers so that we could be next to each other; it was so worth it. Every morning we'd spend the time before class catching up on everything we'd missed over night, as if so much had happened. Now it was just a reminder of something that once was.

The air hit me like a sprayed perfume, filling every section of my nose and lungs with unprecedented force, pushing me backwards. I felt too numb to feel the push, I carried on past it. Voices began to call behind me, but they were blurs. Nothing mattered.

"*We've got this,*" I said to myself.

In my mind I was running, pushing past everything, letting

the air guide my mood. But I was just stumbling, falling over each crutch as I scurried out of school.

"Want a hand?" A sharp voice pierced through the numb shield that weaved around me. I turned to see two students, boy and girl, walking towards me from behind the art block. I knew who they were, but I didn't know them.

"I'm all ri—" I began, stumbling too far. They caught me before I could finish.

"Come," the boy said, putting my arm over his shoulder and pulling me forwards, out of the school gate. He smelt strange: earthy.

"Can you take this?" he asked the girl, handing her my backpack.

"NO!" I screamed, a final attempt to save my parents.

"It's cool." The girl grinned, one hand surrendering. "I won't open it."

They led me towards an old, battered red Ford Fiesta. I sat in the seat without thought, putting my entire trust in two strangers.

The rev of the engine ignited my senses. I looked around, perplexed.

"Who are you?" I choked.

"Ha, of course you wouldn't know who we are," the girl scoffed, her kind tone already changed.

"Jess, be nice!" the boy snapped. I looked at him for the first time. His hair was thick, wavy, and hung loose around his shoulder. A dimple sat either side of a gently crooked smile, his eyes dark and hollow. There was something sweet about him, something mystical; I knew he was trouble.

"I'm sorry," I replied.

"Ignore her, she's just missed her breakfast." He smiled again. I couldn't help but smile back, my throat drying slightly. I thought of Lex. What was I doing here?

"We share every single class together," Jess continued. "...But then you only see who Cally lets you see, isn't that right?"

"Jess, knock it off." He jumped, this time glaring back at her.

She was right; I had no idea who they were. I'd always befriended Cally's friends.

"I…" I began to defend myself, but saw no point. I just stared at the passing fields, lost in humiliation.

"Where are we going?" I asked, noticing the roads leaving town.

"Crow Hill," the boy said. "Don't worry… we wont walk to the top," he continued, noticing my concern at my crutch. "I'm Jake by the way."

The road to Crow Hill was concealed in a sharp turn off the main road. Giant evergreens crowded over the off-road track, clouding the path into darkness. We were all silent, our voices stolen by trees. They pulled the car into a small lay-by area halfway up the hill. We were the only people here. Jake parked and ran around to my door, helping me out of the car. They both set off, walking towards the light that peered through the woods. I hobbled behind. It was beautifully peaceful.

"Do you need a hand?" Jess asked, noticing me stumble.

"Thanks."

Linked into her arms I felt re-assured; it was just like Cally and I.

We reached the vista, overlooking the town below. I walked straight to the edge, staring down at BWC and everything that had changed me. I felt caught in a transient state, the past too raw and the future unknown. Jake and Jess were sat back against a bench, eyes staring at the sky above. I watched as Jess pulled out a long piece of paper, rolled it tight and began to light it. I didn't blink. I looked again; it was a spliff. My stomach burned. I had gone from hell to something I was completely not ready for. I had no idea how to handle it.

The journey back was like an Alton Towers ride I had been nudged onto against my will. My fingers locked around the door handle, anticipating the car flipping over as stoned Jake guided it through the narrow roads. I didn't speak; instead I kept imagining the newspaper spread... THREE INTOXICATED TEENS PLUNGE TO THEIR DEATH IN FATAL ACCIDENT. I gripped the handle tighter.

The bit that got me was that I hadn't done it, yet *I* felt the guilt of a thousand criminals. I had always been under the strong understanding that *Drugs are bad.* I couldn't get my head around when this had changed, and when driving under the influence became a part of everyday life. My stomach started to calm a little, diffusing the fear across my body in flames. I gripped tighter to stop myself exploding, focusing intently on the passing trees as if my gaze could cut them with a laser. My freak-out went entirely unnoticed against the heated frenzy of the now rowdy car.

"Pick you up tomorrow?" Jake giggled, leaning across to open my door. I stared at him, furious. How dare he think I would come on another journey to hell with him? WHO DOES HE THINK I AM? I am Romola Herbert; I would never get into a car again with a known CRIMINAL. As I spun my head away from him towards my house I noticed my mum's car in the driveway. All my anxiety flooded back into its designated stomach spot.

"Sure. Thanks," my humiliated lips replied. Without turning to look at my tempters, I stumbled out of the car.

I have never been scared to go home, it's always been my haven when things got difficult. This had begun to change over the past few years as Mum and Dad's arguments became more regular, but even then, my room was still there for me. Staring at my own front door, I could feel a thick, fuzzy force field around the house, deterring me from entering. Instead I slid down to the floor, sitting and waiting, for something... anything to help my newly confused world. Instead my irrational stomach churned fast below my gut, whisking together all my insecurities.

Half an hour passed and I was still outside the front door, caught in a fierce staring competition with a neighbour's tree. My phone was burning against my leg, messages filling all my social inboxes. We were in twenty-first century England, but still the teenage world was ridden with slimy teenagers who felt the need to feed off other people's torment.

Romola Herbert... how's life in the head teacher's pants?

I scrolled down the vicious comments that were plastered across my phone, but the worst ones were the pity. I fell heavier against the pavement, before I reached a thread from Lex.

Romola, please call me.

Romola... we need to speak.

Where are you?

Are you okay?

I tried to pick myself up again, the messages giving me a little strength in anger. My phone buzzed again.

I'm so sorry, Cally messaged.

The text crumbled my momentary strength... I opened the door and hobbled into my bedroom, where I wept continuously until I fell asleep.

ALEXANDER

The school was whispers. No one seemed to speak for the entire day. News swiftly spread to Mr Thompson, the head teacher, who refused to look at anyone – student or teacher – in the face. The teachers looked like students, exchanging unprofessional looks and comments when they passed each other. Alice Jennings was sent home immediately, when the deputy head had investigated the leak. Romola was nowhere to be seen.

"Alexander," Cally wailed down the corridor at lunch. "Have you spoken to her?"

"I've tried calling," I replied, ashamed of my dire attempt at contact.

"Same. I even skipped last period to check at home but she wasn't there. I have no idea where she's gone."

"Look, Cally, I have no fucking idea, okay?" I snapped back. "You'll have to try someone else."

I walked away and headed to the canteen to join the lads, who had already moved on from this morning to discuss other sports-related issues. I was more comfortable here, like this. I could be one of them and that was easier.

"OI! You coming tonight, Alex?" Jed called over the table. "School social?"

I nodded, shaking off this morning and messing around with the lads as they discussed what alcohol to score for the evening.

I arranged to pick Alice up at eight.

ROMOLA

I woke an hour later to a spinning room; my heart was thumping in my chest and stomach aching with acidic burn. I felt a little delirious, wondering if I had dreamt everything I could remember. I sat up gradually, taking in the surroundings of my bedroom. It all looked so normal, nothing had changed since this morning. I was certain I could've dreamt it all. Until I glanced at the slightly torn rucksack at the foot of my bed, spilling out A4 sheets of paper, covered with my family's disgrace.

I couldn't be in the room any longer. I slipped on some fresh clothes and a new face of make up and headed out the door. No idea where I was going, I began to hobble on my crutches. I had never been humiliated before, not like this. The whole event was a little ridiculous, heart breaking and eternally damaging for my family. Surely it was not enough to condemn me as an eternal loser at school? Within a couple of minutes I had called a taxi and was on route to the social. I was determined to show my face and not allow this event to traumatise the rest of my secondary school year. I didn't honestly believe that people were so cruel as to shame me for something like this. I was utterly wrong.

As I walked up the path towards the house I realised I really had never been there. It was a huge house that belonged to one of the guys on the football team, whose parents were always away for work. I don't know if they knew these events took place every week, but if they did, they definitely ignored it. As I got closer to the gate there were groups of students walking around the side of the property onto a narrow off-road path. I decided to follow them, although much slower and often losing sight as the path meandered. The road felt like it went on forever, crowded on one side by tall silver birch trees and a field on the other. The groups ahead were completely out of sight, only the loud sound of music guiding me onwards.

Behind me I could hear the distant sound of cars getting closer. I shuffled my way behind a tree, embarrassed to be alone, desperately trying to hide against the narrow trunk. Three cars screeched past, the second car slowing a little as it rocked over a small hole in the road, giving me just enough time to see who was inside. I squeezed myself in smaller and clenched my fingers over my stomach as it sunk, at the sight of Lex with Alice. The car manoeuvred and sped off towards the music. I stood still, unsure whether to head home, stay still or push forward. Once again I found myself feeling sickly anxious and incredibly foolish.

Ten minutes passed before my strength urged me to try again. Perhaps I needed answers; could I honestly believe that on this day especially, he would be with her? I couldn't trust my own eyes, my sanity or my clenched stomach.

The last part of the walk seemed to go fast, too fast perhaps. I found myself standing at the entrance to a huge, American-style barn, clutching the handle to enter. There were small staggered groups of smokers chuckling outside, although I took comfort for the first time in the fact that their humour was smoke-induced and not at me. With one hand clutched around the door and the other to balance myself, I pulled the door open and looked in.

The entire top three years of school seemed to be in the barn. I could hardly believe I had never been. The room was full of lights, spread across the ceiling, that made me sure his parents either knew about the parties or this barn was used for other occasions. It was magical and warming, like somewhere I had dreamed of attending. My life up until now had only consisted of family occasions and the odd wedding when I was too small to remember. This was beautifully designed with tall drapes of linen sweeping across the walls. For a moment I thought I was trespassing on someone's party, but the picture of Lex and Alice clung in my mind. Even with all the splendour of the room, I felt cold and nervous.

I looked around at all the familiar faces engrossed in conversation. They howled as loud as their mouths would allow them without spitting too much drink on their converser. No one noticed me as I stood at the door, all far too intoxicated to feel the cold air enter the hall. Or perhaps they noticed but simply didn't care. I began scanning the room for Lex. I needed to be sure I had seen what I thought I had seen.

I picked up my crutch that had been resting against the door and started into the room. It was either the sound of the clutch moving against the barn door or me being in closer proximity, but the entire room started to look at me. I couldn't help wondering if a message had flooded the inboxes of everyone in the room or a ripple of words had travelled before I took the step. But that was just my paranoia. It was obvious, no one had forgotten this morning and nor had I.

I shook it off, my stomach battling my adrenaline and urging me into the room. As I passed, each student looked at me and then back to the group they were with – a little grimace being shared between.

At the edge of the room was a long table filled with an array of snacks and alcohol. I headed over and poured myself the largest alcoholic drink I could and began to chug it down quickly and effortlessly. I had never really drunk before, just the occasional small glass at a family event or a silly glass with Cally. This was going to hit me so hard but I didn't care. I wanted for one night to be normal, to attend the social, to get drunk like everyone else and be fake happy like everyone else. I wanted it so bad – until I saw them together.

It wasn't long after I had finished the glass of vodka and orange that I began to stumble around the room looking for him. In my already vodka-induced haze I felt determined to see Lex – the only person I could see. I was eager to see him – excited even. In that moment I could conquer anything – all anxiety. I felt myself gliding through the room and everything falling away, I almost couldn't feel the crutches in my hand. It was all too fast, too quick and too painful.

He was with Alice, gathered in a group at the back of the barn. They were all laughing and joking, like everything was normal. My paranoia felt mocked. I wondered if it had all been a dream – to socialise so freely with the girl who had disgraced my family – it must have been a dream. But as I moved closer I saw more. I saw girls huddled in corners with guys, the laughs were occasional and the air was hot. Lex was not talking to Alice but caught tangled in a deep embrace, lips plastered across hers like their air was one. It was everything and nothing, heated and horrible. I felt sick. My stomach layered with acid and my chest burnt with toxic fluid. This wasn't just the vodka, but the built-up energy of embarrassment, fear… and betrayal.

I turned before they could see me and began to head out of the barn, but couldn't make it.

This was by far the worst social event of my entire life. My stomach was filled with burns and throat thick with mucus. I believe it was the physical torment that led me to do what I did next. Perhaps a little part of me enjoyed it, a two-fingers-up to everyone there. I could feel the tears pulsing behind my eyelids; I was desperate to not let them fall. Perhaps it was the tears then, but whatever provoked it, it was unavoidable.

Something inside me couldn't be defeated. I wanted to feel, to experience something real. So I stopped and stared. I watched the teenagers eagerly kissing in front of me with laughter and joy. I watched others ahead of me dancing together and choking back their drinks. I saw the ease of their moves and listened to the rhythm of the music. I wanted to be them – anyone but myself.

A moment later I was dancing, tears poured out of my eyes with uncontrollable will. The past few weeks of loneliness urged me to sob. The past few hours of learning about my parents cut so deep I could feel the bad energy leak through my eyes. The past few seconds seeing Lex with *her*, made the uncontrollable sobs paint my face with the pathetic desperation of a girl utterly lost. And yet I still danced, alone and confused.

I could've stayed there for ages, eyes closed and lost in my thoughts. Yet like hounds released from a cage, the whispers began to bark, the laughs began to direct and the eyes were watching me. I didn't need to look to know that I was the subject of their humour, but I did. I looked and saw the humiliation, I *should've* been feeling, in their eyes. I saw the stupidity they saw when they looked at me, plastered across their laughing faces. I saw Lex making his way towards me, so I ran as fast as my crutched legs would let me.

ALEXANDER

Alice was silent when I picked her up. It was clear she was cautious of me, surprised even to see me at her door. I had no idea why I was there either. She climbed into the car seat barely looking at me. I barely looked at her. She pulled out her phone and was texting people the entire way to the social. I was used to this with Elle: every journey, date or moment together was like this. I was thankful Alice was distracted. As we neared the barn the music pulled her away from her phone and her face brightened at the prospect of the night. I caught her gaze for a moment but darted my eyes away. Until that moment I hadn't even admitted to myself that I was angry with Alice, disgusted even.

The road was dark, with only the occasional car headed to the same place and one approaching behind. It all felt quite surreal, like the world was resuming. This was to most people just any Friday night. I slowed the car a little, noticing a girl huddled behind a tree. Her back faced us and the dark obscured her enough that I couldn't make out her face. She reminded me a little of Romola, and with that thought I sped off, leaving her alone behind the tree. I was a coward. It felt physical, like a force in my body holding me back and preventing me from doing the right thing. I knew what I should be doing, but fear stuck to my chest like a burden.

"Quick, we'll be late," Alice nudged, breaking me away

from my thoughts. I was thankful for the distraction, so smiled and put my foot down on the pedal. She noticed the corner of my lips rise a little and relaxed her shoulders immediately, as though the air had been cleared.

The field behind the barn was full of cars. I parked as close to the gate as possible so that I could leave early. I wasn't going to drink and barely wanted to be here at all. I felt like a corpse, being pulled to entertain.

These events were always the same. Usually I enjoyed them, just to see everyone laughing and to dance to some ridiculous songs. The guys were always planning some prank or would gather at the back of the barn to drink and laugh. Tonight was different; everyone was paired up or grouped. Alcohol was being chucked around like there was no tomorrow and the stench of weed filled the entrance.

"Hey, Alex!" Jed beckoned. "Game of pool, mate?"

"Sure."

Jed always smashed everyone at pool until I arrived back to challenge his title. Every week he attempted to re-claim himself.

"This will be the niiiggghyaattt!" he snorted.

"You wish." I laughed, jabbing him in the side before he could guard himself.

Alice scoffed and shrugged her shoulders, walking into the barn to join some other girls.

My head wasn't in the game. My fingers started to slip as Jed chanted across the table.

"Mate, I'm gonna smash you. Where you at?"

I shrugged.

"You were bound to beat me soon," I half-laughed as he potted the last ball.

"YAYYYEERRRRRRR!" he belted, walking like a chicken

in a victory dance. "You've been slaughtered."

She came in like darkness, quick and without warning. I couldn't see or feel anything, but kiss her back as her big lips pressed against mine. Her chest pushed against me and I felt myself floating backwards until I touched the wall behind. It was cold and hard. I lost myself for a moment: the victorious teenage boy triumphant in his score. The music sounded louder, like my senses were pulled over me. In this moment everything was forgotten and I was just Alex. It was easy and this was why I did it. This was why I always chose her. Alice was the pill to my emotion, the numbing gentle nothingness that I always needed. It had become addictive.

Minutes later and we hadn't stopped kissing, perhaps even intensified. I couldn't see anyone, my eyes were closed and I didn't want to. I heard a cry ahead of me. One by one my senses came back, like adrenaline kicking me into consciousness. I pushed her away and stared into the face of Alice Jennings, her perfectly proportioned features glistening back at me affectionately, but I felt nothing for her.

I could hear the sobbing again, louder this time like a piercing pain in my chest. No one else seemed concerned; no one else heard it. I pushed Alice back slightly with two hands.

"This isn't working," I blurted, moving away just before her mouth dropped and brow furrowed.

"It's not working?" she shouted after me, the entire room turning and clearly hearing that cry.

As I pushed through the crowds in the middle of the room I saw her dancing there. The familiar cry of Romola Herbert was sobbing in front of me like the small girl I used to tease. I felt frozen in time, caught between the past and present. I wanted to go to her and comfort her and apologise. But like then I was responsible for all the pain in front of me. I was the coward who wouldn't act. Some part of me was channeling its way through my body, urging me to move, to run to her. Yet I stayed still. I couldn't breathe or move. I burrowed my head and stared at the transfixed feet below me. Finally I looked up, but she was gone.

ROMOLA

There are two types of anxiety I experience; *social anxiety* and *relationships*, and they both affect my stomach. It all begins like this, heart pounding, stomach burning. Eventually the heat spreads through my blood, like fire weighing down my body. I ache heavily for it to end. My stomach eventually erupts causing me to vomit or worse. This graphic description is the heartfelt cry of my stomach and I.

"Romy." Mum's voice woke me, thumping all my fears against my stomach like a lightening rod. I couldn't move, still in yesterday's clothes on my bed covers.

"Romy, can we talk?" she called again. She knew… of course she knew… the whole town probably knew.

I could hear a thick sadness in her voice, as though she'd been crying. My chest tightened. I couldn't speak to her.

She stayed there for a while, speechless, with just the sound of her heavy breathing against the door. It was a sound that had not so long ago comforted me when I was scared, yet now it sounded a world away from me.

I grabbed my crutch and began to undress. The last thing I could face today was school, but I couldn't stay here either.

A little while later, the sound of a car horn made me flinch. It was Jake. I grabbed my bag and stumbled my way out of the house.

"Morning." Jake grinned.

"Where's Jess?" I asked, noticing the empty seat.

His grin spread wide across his face.

"She's gone to school."

"... And we're not?" I asked, a little confused.

"I had a feeling you might not want to?" he said, shifting in his seat, momentarily uncomfortable.

A pang of panic shivered across my arms... what was I doing? I had never missed a day of school, aside from the accident.

"Where are we going?" I mumbled, not fully agreeing to his plan. Like a second personality, a slight grin peeled across my face. My joker side, the life of the party, was desperate to be promoted from under-study. I wiped it away with a cough.

"How are your legs?" he asked, avoiding the question.

"They're manageable. So where are we going?"

"Out of town."

"You're really not going tell me?" I said.

He shook his head and smiled a new smile; this one was young and sweet. I could see a kindness in him, separate to the tough persona he displayed daily.

"I need to go somewhere first," I added.

It was silent, with only a few cars and elderly walkers out that early on a weekday morning. It was strange being back there with Jake. I was slowly realising that Crow Hill felt a little like the place I ran to. In a strange way it had always been my safe space... well the cafe at least. It was too early to be open now but I knew Liam was baking the daily bread.

I banged on the door a few times before Liam came to open it. His hair was messy and his eyes tired.

"Romola, what's up?"

He looked bewildered, but I couldn't tell if his question was genuine, or a clever way of provoking me to talk. He leaned against the doorframe to steady himself; the fresh dewy air too heavy for his delirious head.

"I don't know, Liam," I replied, biting back the tears that clung to the back of my throat.

He gestured for me to go inside. Without thinking twice about Jake waiting, I followed him into the bakery. It was roasting inside, a sharp change from the crisp morning we had just left. The air was thick with the sweet dark smells of freshly baked bread. It was like coming home, but I had never realised it before. I had never been to the bakery before opening, but the warm smells always travelled up to the cafe, filling the air with delicious reminders throughout the morning.

"This is pretty early for you," he joked, trying to encourage me to talk.

"I know. I don't really know why I'm here. I just kind of ended up here."

Liam laughed a little. I looked up at him to see his cheeky face smiling wearily at me.

"Do you know?" I asked, but as soon as I said it I knew he did.

"Jenny's younger sister told us a little about what had happened. I was going to come to see you, but I figured you'd need space."

There was something about this that infuriated me. Was it really for me that he hadn't come, or was it easier that way? Liam was like a brother to me. We'd been there for each other through so many big conversations. Things changed a little when he got more serious with Jenny, but we still made time to talk when things were important. It bewildered me that anyone would think to give someone space when her world was crashing down; especially when that someone was me.

"Fuck, Liam. YOU KNEW?"

I stood up, my head spinning slightly as I shot up too fast.

"Only recently, Romy. I'm sorry, I thought it was best to stay away."

"Best for who, Liam?"

I didn't wait for him to reply. I hobbled out of the bakery, blocking his final words with the sound of each crutch. I don't think I would've made sense of them if I'd heard them, everything felt hazy. It was as though the world had fallen and I realised just how utterly alone I really was.

And then I saw Jake.

"Wasn't one fall enough for you?" Jake laughed, trying to lift me as I stumbled back to the car, my legs weaker from the fear. He smelled strange, like a mixture of burnt leaves and musk; the earthy smell of cannabis lingering on his jacket. It made me want to gag a little, but the softness of his grasp was so comforting that I let my body fall into his.

"Thank you," I mumbled.

"Are you ready now?" he asked as he climbed into his seat. I had no idea where we were going but I knew that I wanted to get as far away from here as I could.

"Okay."

Leaving town felt like we were never going to return. The weight of the past glued itself to the leaving sign. As we reached the motorway I began to feel a little more like myself again.

"I'm guessing you know?" I asked, watching Jake's reaction carefully.

"That your folks are a little rocky?" he finished with a shrug. "I guess that's pretty normal."

I couldn't believe how easily he dismissed it. Part of me was a little offended but it felt like the world had been re-aligned momentarily. In this car I could be normal. BETTER. I could be anyone I wanted to be. Jake had no idea who I really was and I don't think he cared. This was a chance to re-create myself. No fears, no weaknesses.

I had fallen asleep. The gentle murmur of the car engine reminded me we were driving. I shifted to look at Jake; his long blonde hair was pulled back into a bun. Watching him through one eye, he looked so calm and normal. His jaw was strong and more evident with his hair up. I sat up, rubbing my eyes. Two hours had passed.

"Where are we?" I asked, this time a little concerned.

"My parents have a house down here."

"Where is here?"

"The coast."

ALEXANDER

I avoided school the next day. Mum said nothing. It wasn't like I often decided not to go, so she just seemed to accept it.

Confusion sat next to me all day, wrapping insecurity in my thoughts. There were times where I concluded that I was mentally unwell. It wasn't a gentle mental depravity I spoke about. I wasn't anxious or depressed. I couldn't help wondering if I was split into two. The only rational reasoning for acting this way would be if I were unwell. I spent the day trawling the internet for cases of MPD (Multiple Personality Disorder) but they all seemed to be triggered by a tragic event. They were usually very different and felt like numerous personalities, whereas I had just two. I could attempt to hide behind the idea that I suffered with MPD but in fact I was just a teenage boy battling with the reality that I was a coward.

"Hey, mate, is everything okay?"

Dad called in the evening, when it had become too apparent for Mum to ignore the fact that I wasn't planning on going to school in the near future.

"Uh, yeah," I replied normally.

"So, you gonna get yourself to school tomorrow?" he mumbled.

"Yeah," I said.

There were of course perks of years spent crafting how to fake a personality. It was easy to fool anyone, even your parents.

I sometimes wondered if they knew, but it was easier this way to avoid a conversation. Mum always had her own concerns and Dad was too busy to deal with my shit.

"Great, son." He brightened on the phone. "See you next weekend then."

And just like that the phone conversation was finished.

I left the house the next morning, completely numb. It was as though the entire emotional section of my brain was switching off. I kept walking for hours, going nowhere in particular. At one point I ended up on Crow Hill staring down at the town below. I used to come here every weekend with my parents; we'd get to the top and scream. Well now I think about it, I screamed, they laughed.

I stayed there for a couple of hours before making my way down into town. It was pretty empty, but that was usual for a small town like this. The city was always buzzing; it was so much easier to disappear.

"All right, Alex." A guy nodded as he passed me. I barely knew him, but that was the thing about being the new person at school, everyone knew me. Let alone the fact I was the only black kid in my year.

"S'up." I nodded normally.

The small moment of human interaction pulled me out of my numbness for a second as I realised where I was. I had walked to Romola's house. The outside was calm but the drawn curtains were strange, like the house was hiding something. Guilt flooded into my chest like an intense wave of heat. For a moment it was all I could feel, prickling down my nerves to the ends of my fingers. I watched the house waiting for it to move, to awake me from this feeling. It was easier to feel nothing; I preferred that.

Minutes later I was still standing in the same spot. I imagined the curtains being pulled across and her sweet face scowling at me through the windows. She had always made me feel something. Even as young kids, her anger and red face made me feel alive. Looking at her windows, all I felt was intense guilt.

The next thing I was running.

"Shit, Alex." She laughed. "I thought you were done."

But I didn't reply, I just kissed her.

"Seriously, though." She pushed me away. "You're such a dick."

I had waited outside school for Alice and pulled her aside to talk to her. I didn't have anything to say, so I just kissed her. She kissed me back for a while, before reason swept across her face. I had gone too far this time; I knew that.

"I screwed up," I replied, staring straight into her big eyes. She was so perfect, her brows forming gentle arches and her lips bouncing up at the centre. I leant in to kiss her again; this always worked with Elle.

"Yeah, you did." Alice punched me in the arm. "You fucking did."

She moved me aside, flicking her hair off her shoulder slightly as she walked away. The strange thing was I couldn't figure out which part I had screwed up the most, Alice or Romola. Or at least which one bothered me more.

I didn't feel anything. I just stood there watching her leave, shrugged slightly and walked off to the football pitch.

"You playing, mate?" Jed nodded, clearly unaffected by the fact I had half-dumped his sister on the weekend.

"Nah, mate, I'm gonna sit this one out."

The news echoed across school, through the corridors, playground, down the netball courts to the football field. It came like a soft rattle, shaking each person one at a time. First they looked up, leaned in; their hands went to their mouths or jaws fell. Then they would turn, lean and whisper again to someone else. Watching it channel down felt like a wave at a football game, you waited a little nervous that you would miss it when it finally arrived at you. I could feel it heating up my blood, like my secret being shared across the field. There would be the occasional glance at me before they turned to share the message again. It was this look that made me certain that I had been outed; someone knew I was a fraud. Could Alice have told everyone already that I'd kissed her, would she really want to tell everyone? I knew it wasn't that, I knew that wouldn't be enough for this. There was also no way they could ever know about what was going on in my head, and yet I knew this was personal. In moments like this I felt everything. I knew now that I cared just a bit too much.

"Fuck, Alex, have you heard?"

It was my time now, to turn, lean and look shocked. I didn't want to.

There is something about gossip, you will observe it for yourself; it cannot be ignored. I wonder if it is a part of the brain that is programmed to want to know or desperate to tell. As I looked up now everyone was looking at me. They were waiting for something.

"Romola's been missing for two days."

The words rang through my body like a defibrillator awakening my nerves. I shot up. There wasn't a face not watching now, all the matches had stopped. I could see guilt spread across them all, each one that had laughed, ignored or gossiped. I couldn't look at them, because they echoed myself.

"What the fuck?" I managed to spit back at Jed.

"That's all I know." He shrugged, leaving to return to the match. One by one his movements encouraged the flock to turn back to their lives. There were the few that took longer, still shocked by the news. The volume rose again as whispers began to spread bad information and unknown conclusions.

ROMOLA

The house was huge and magnificently beautiful. As I climbed out, I took another look at the beaten-up car he was driving and back at the red-brick manor house in front of me. Greenery climbed up the pillared doorway inviting you into the house. The windows were framed in elegant carvings with old-fashioned glass paneling. It was like stepping back in time.

"You're rich?" I blurted. "You don't act like it!"

He burst out laughing, like he'd been holding back in so many ways.

"My parents are rich," he added.

"That's what all rich people say!" I laughed, following him towards the house.

"You hungry?" He was holding the door for me.

"So hungry!" I replied, realising the true extent of my hunger as my stomach grumbled in response. We both laughed a little. As I looked at him, I caught his eye and felt awkward for a moment. I shook it off and moved further into the house. The doors opened onto a tall hallway with marble checkered floors and the longest stone staircase.

"You're really rich!" I blurted again, uncontrollably.

He guided me into the kitchen, placing his hand on my back as I hobbled slightly.

"Let me see what we have." He nodded, sitting me on a bar stool in his gigantic kitchen and moving towards the fridge. The kitchen was styled in traditional English countryside aesthetic with a modern twist that made you feel like you'd seen it in a World of Interiors magazine. He pulled open the large fridge door to countless fully stocked shelves.

"Are we not alone?" I asked.

"Um, no we are alone. I was already planning on coming down here so my parents got some food sent in."

As he said it, it was a though we both realised that we were alone in this huge house. I had never really been alone with a guy, other than Lex. The strangest thing is I didn't feel anxious at all. My stomach grumbled with hunger but it was calm.

"Do you mind?" he asked, watching my eyes flicker as I thought.

"Uh." It took me a second to remember what he was referring to. "Um no, I don't mind." I smiled. As I said it I was reminded that I really didn't know Jake at all. It was a little crazy to have followed him hours across England. I probably should've called my parents right then, but I was still angry with them.

"You okay?" Jake asked, standing beside me, his hand resting on my shoulder. It wasn't until he spoke that I realised I was crying. My hands were drenched in liquid and cheeks inflamed at the thought of my mum.

"Oh, yeah, I'm okay." I shrugged him off, embarrassed by the sympathy. "Thanks for the food." I smiled weakly, taking a bite out of the sandwich he had prepared in front of me.

"So how many rooms does this house have?" I grinned, changing the subject. "It's like a palace!"

"You wanna see?"

The house had ten bedrooms, a library, a games room, a swimming pool, tennis courts and endless corridors. It was a paradise and completely surreal.

"What do your parents do?" I asked, when we had finally planted ourselves on a sofa in a living room. Jake looked away, clearly wishing to avoid conversations like this.

"My dad works in the City," he replied. "My mum doesn't work."

He shifted in his seat and it was clear he didn't want to talk about this any more.

"What about yours?" he added, before seeing me squirm a little. "Shit, sorry. I forgot for a second, you wouldn't want to talk about that."

"No, it's fine." I shrugged. "My dad and mum work... well worked... or work – I have no idea what will happen, in their construction company."

He looked uncomfortable, shifting around in his seat.

"Did you know?" he added.

"That my mum was a slut?" I scoffed, louder and more forceful than I intended. "No, I didn't know."

"Sorry." He looked away ashamed.

"No, it's fine. I just don't know if I want to talk or not. Part of me wants to shout about it and cry and laugh. It all feels so ridiculous. Part of me isn't surprised either. But it's just so humiliating!"

He was watching me carefully.

"They've been arguing for years, so I guess I knew they'd divorce. An affair, though, that was just too much. I don't think I'll ever forgive her."

We were silent for a while. I stared out the window into the garden and Jake played with his hoodie zip.

"Fuck, I hate parents," he shouted.

We looked at each other and burst out laughing.

ALEXANDER

When I arrived at the house, Mum was already there with Mrs Herbert. They both looked faint, like they had both lost a child.

"Alexander," Mum shouted when she saw me. "Come here now!"

She sounded exasperated, gesturing her arm towards me in a sharp pointed wave. When I reached her she pulled me in close and hugged me like she had never hugged me before. It felt strange and unfamiliar, but I let it happen.

"Is it true?" I coughed through the embrace. "Is she really gone?"

She pulled away and nodded, looking over at Romola's mum as she did.

"She hasn't been in contact for a couple of days now."

Two policemen came out of the house with her father, nodding and talking quietly with them both before they left.

"Alexander!" Mr Herbert called when he saw me, pulling me away from my mum into his own embrace. "Have you heard from her?"

I shook my head.

"Okay." He pulled away from me, a little disappointed.

"What's happening?" I managed to ask without exploding, my entire body felt sick.

"We assumed she was in her room." He looked cautiously at me. "I know it's a terrible thing to say, but it wasn't like we thought she would be far. The girl can barely walk." He choked as he said it, reminded of her depraved situation.

"We thought she needed space." He sighed. "After everything."

"Alexander, you need to call her yourself." Mum gestured to my pocket, where my phone was sticking out slightly. I nodded and did what she asked, without admitting that I'd been calling non-stop on the way over. The truth was that every second I wasn't trying to call her, I felt my entire body attempting to seizure.

"There's nothing," I shouted, startling everyone as I became unable to hide my anger.

"Fuck this!" I shouted again.

"ALEXANDER!" Mum scowled at me.

"No, it's fine," Mr Herbert replied, attempting to make reassuring gestures with his hands, but just flapping them around without purpose. "It's fine," he repeated over a few times, before falling to his knees and weeping.

It's a strange thing to watch a man cry. You quickly become aware of the space around you, like everything wakes up. The bodies all around were like firm statues, afraid to move even for a moment in disturbance. Watching Mr Herbert break down was like watching his entire existence shatter into a thousand pieces beside him. I knew that if I didn't attempt to scoop them up, he would be eternally lost. Without a moment's thought I went to him and hugged him. It was strange to be close to someone else, let alone a man who was very much a father figure to me. I can't remember the last time I even looked at my own dad properly.

"We will find her," I reassured him uncertainly.

A few minutes later and my mum had taken them both into the house. I stood there motionless for a while, perplexed and unable to move. I had always thought it ridiculous that in a state of emergency people are frozen, but here in that moment it was impossible to move. My mind was fuelled by action, calculating all the ways I could attempt to find her, but my body just wouldn't shift. Eventually I pulled out my phone and scanned social media for any hints on her whereabouts.

"Cally," I called into the phone, pressing it harder into my ear in an attempt to encourage the desirable reply, "have you spoken to her?"

"No," she sobbed. "I don't know what to do."

"Meet me in fifteen?" I replied. "I'll come to you."

I had no idea what we would do, but I figured we could cover more ground together. Romola's parents had been told to stay home by the police, in case she returned; but there was no way I could sit still.

ROMOLA

Being with Jake felt like anything we did here wouldn't count. It was a free card to not care about anything; something I hadn't felt the liberty of before. Here there were no parents watching over me, no friends calling and nothing to remind me of the person I should be. Life until now had felt as though I were taking every step with a harness strapped to my shoulders.

I hardly even knew Jake and that excited me. He was the one who was unpredictable and it was a freedom that wasn't my concern. It was like taking all the inward fury and watching it spin in front of my eyes. He was the energetic chaos from within and I could just watch it unravel without responsibility. I felt full of youth.

I hadn't seen my parents since Saturday, having spent Sunday ignoring them and leaving on Monday morning. I felt the guilt ripping across my stomach at the thought of them concerned, and yet I was enjoying it. My acid-ridden stomach was comforted by the idea that for once I was forced into their front mirror. When they woke up and wondered where I was, I enjoyed the thought that they couldn't be selfish for just once. It was my turn to be the centre, my turn to have problems. In this moment, I hated them so much. The hate felt so raw; it was stricken with fear, which I nudged lower, until the worry just numbed my anxious stomach.

"You up?" Jake called though the door as I began getting dressed. "Do you want breakfast?"

"Yes! I'm up and that would be amazing," I called back.

I clenched my stomach as I spoke; the mornings were always the worst. Usually I hadn't slept well during the night, giving plenty of time for acid to build. Today was different. I had slept all night without waking, in the most surreal and deep sleep. As I stood staring at my reflection in the mirror, the nerves flooded in with the blood rushing eagerly to my toes. The girl in front of me was identical to the person who I'd left behind. I knew now that no matter how far away I was, it would always be me staring back.

"Here, I made pancakes." Jake grinned as I hobbled into the kitchen. "Do you like fruit or just maple?"

"Wow!" I laughed. "I'll have anything."

I felt strangely calm around Jake, in a way I had never felt around Lex. It struck my insides even to think it, so I brushed it off.

"These are amazing!" I mumbled through a mouthful of pancakes.

"Thanks. They're about the only thing I can cook." He grinned, locking with my eyes for a moment too long.

He was attractive, in a less obvious way. His hair was always messy and his clothes rough, which was peculiar knowing what his house looked like. His lips were such a deep pink and his eyes a sweet blue that made him seem sweetly kind. I found myself watching him long after our eyes detached. Feeling my gaze, he ran his fingers slowly through his hair, now sitting gently at the curve of his jaw. There was something mischievous in his manner, as though he knew I was watching him and wanted to encourage me, so I played along and continued for a little longer.

"So, are you dating Alex?" he blurted, turning to look at me directly.

I was startled; I choked on my pancake and burst out laughing.

"No way! Why?" I asked.

I don't know why I was so surprised. Maybe it was the thought of me being with Lex or disbelief that someone thought he would choose to be with me. Perhaps it was a bit of both.

"It was just something being said at school."

"Wow, things really spread," I scoffed bitterly.

"You're close though, right?" he continued, clearly not giving up that easily.

"Yeah, well, kind of." I looked away as I spoke, guilt residing in my stomach. "Our families are close."

I felt strange talking about Lex to Jake.

"Do you know him?" I added, sensing something in the way Jake spoke about Lex that was different. He drifted off for a moment, caught in a thought or contemplating how to answer.

"Fuck, no. I don't know anyone." He sniggered. "He seems all right though, just not sure about the ones he's close to."

We both laughed as he realised what he'd insinuated.

"Not you, of course."

"Totally."

"Can you swim?" he asked, filling up my coffee cup for the second time.

"Normally. But I haven't attempted to since the accident."

"What's up with that now? Are you almost healed?"

I looked down at my legs and the crutches beside them.

"Almost, my legs are just weaker now."

"Sweet. That must've been intense."

"Yep, just a little." I laughed at his ease of dismissal. Everything sounded so easy with Jake, like nothing would ever be a big deal.

"So can you brave the sea?"

"I can brave the beach."

It was strange being at the seaside with Jake, having only recently been with Lex. The English coast always looked similar. The heavy waves pushed by the autumn winds and bright skies are deceptive of the cold weather.

"Are you going in?" I asked Jake as he slipped off his trousers and shirt to reveal a wetsuit underneath.

"If you don't mind?"

"No, go!"

He left me stationed on a picnic blanket in the only sunny spot on the beach. Strapped to his car roof was a surfboard that I hadn't noticed before. Within minutes Jake and the board were in the sea. It was the first time I had truly felt content being alone. Throughout the past few months I was always desperate to be out of the house or for Lex to be with me. I even felt a craving for Mum and Dad's attention when I was lacking any other. Now it was complete peace. Everything was still and I took a large inhale, waiting for the thick salty air to expand as I exhaled. It was easy here.

I took out my phone to look at it; it was an impulse reaction. I'd become so used to checking it for social media. Staring at the dark screen now I realised I hadn't even looked at it since we arrived. Attempting to switch it on, the button stuck and the battery was flat. A pang of sickness shredded through my stomach. It was strange to think that I could feel anything within this clouded heaviness that was permanently residing there. It was as though anxiety was sitting there to keep me weighted, but when that wasn't enough, my demon would strike. I could feel it heating, the sharp bites of fear shooting up my throat in hot gulps. I was panting, trying desperately to take a breath but drowning on land.

Responsibility is a strange witness; there are moments where you believe it isn't there. Those blissful fragments that make you feel like you can just drop everything and be free. It is a bittersweet trickery because when responsibility is chronically in your blood, you can't flout it even for a moment.

I tried to relax again, to tell myself over and over that it was okay to have no communication. I had wanted my parents to worry; that was the point of this, right?

Instead I forced myself to watch the sea, to see Jake play with the tides. He was so carefree in everything that he did; I wondered how it was so easy for him. Closing my eyes, I leant back and slept against the blanket.

"Do you want some?"

I was startled by the voice but firstly by the sickly damp smell of the joint.

"Fuck, no," I spat at him, jolting up and away from the nauseating smell.

"Do you have to smoke it here?" I said, pretending to gag, whilst honestly trying to compose my already temperamental stomach.

"You hate it." He laughed whilst taking another drag. It was that mocking laugh that people typically make when they're enjoying a 'controversial' pastime. It was the kind of laugh that sits with you for a moment as your eyes dart back and forth to assess the judgment.

"I hate the smell," I lied, desperately not wanting to tell him how the mere thought of doing something illegal like that made my insides burn harder. "Besides, I don't want to like it."

Jake shrugged. He wasn't like most people when you tell them you're not into drugs. It had become a real thing at school in the past year, especially weed. Inevitably I had found myself in the situation twice now where I'd had to turn away and say no. The first time it was easy, those sweet childlike morals were enough for me to sharply reply. It might've been the same the second time but for the laughter that came in response to my objection. It was a repetitive sound, like someone who can't finish a laugh so they just 'ha' over and over and over until you question your entire existence along with your desire to smoke. The second time I was asked I replied short, sweet and nonchalant. That barely worked. But Jake didn't seem to care at all. It was so matter of fact, that I didn't even mind him smoking next to me. It was as though our views were truly insignificant or perhaps so significant their presence wasn't wanted now.

"I used to come here as a kid with my dad," Jake began slowly. He stubbed out the joint as he spoke, which I was thankful for, to avoid any further stench. "It was my favourite place to be; it still is I guess. Don't you think it's strange how trivial life becomes as you grow older and how important everything seems as kid?"

He didn't wait for me to interject.

"Like the rock pools; they were so exciting and we'd spend hours searching for creatures as though that moment were everything. Now, everything just seems to be waiting for something else to happen. Do you get that?"

It was strange how open he felt, I couldn't tell if it was the marijuana or his temperament. It made me feel strangely okay, like I could relax again. I lay back and looked up at the sky as he spoke.

"I guess so. Things were definitely more simple before."

"It's like the world just fucks up when you grow up."

He began to laugh as though he'd said something so profound and startled himself. I replayed his words in my head to assess their worth before joining into his endless giggles. Everything here felt still, and that was all I needed.

ALEXANDER

"What would she do?" I asked Cally as we began to drive. I had no idea where to drive to, nothing I knew about Romola from before would be relevant to her life today.

"I don't know. She doesn't know anyone other than us."

"There must be somewhere she would go when shit happens," I said angrily. There was a strange protectiveness in my body; I could feel it tensing in preparation.

"We could try Beanies or Liam."

"Liam? Who's that?" A shudder of jealousy found its way into my stomach. It was unwelcome and unfamiliar to feel an emotion so direct.

"Liam's her guy friend." She was watching me as she said it, quickly adding, "Before you, I mean, after you. Wait, what even are you guys?"

I didn't answer her.

Beanies was different to the shack that stood in its place before we moved. Then it was a simple wooden building with a few scattered benches outside. It was always swarming with people on the weekends; families ready to climb the hill with their breakfast in hand. It was strange being back here and everything was changed, even the reference to Romola here was different. This was her place, a life after me. Of course I knew she'd been living, but naively I wished she hadn't. There was something comforting in fooling myself that she was an outsider with little going on. It made my sad existence for the past years more acceptable, like our lives would resume at the same time.

"So she worked here?" I bit down on my lip, trying to shake off my selfish jealousy.

"Every weekend. She loved it here."

We headed into the cafe; a decent sized cabin with tables inside and shelves full of fresh produce on the one side. It was cute and quirky, completely Romola.

"Hi, Camilla," Jan shouted as soon as she saw us coming in. The cafe was closed and confused customers stood outside contemplating their change of plans.

"Camilla?" I repeated, glaring at Cally, who shot me back a look of trust.

"Is there any news?" Jan panted desperately.

"Nothing. We were hoping you might know something."

"Only what Liam told the police."

I shot up again, the tension spreading into my shoulders.

"What did he tell them?" She looked a little confused to hear me be so direct. It reminded me that we were strangers caught in a panicked moment.

"They only recently left, so I guess it hasn't travelled that fast yet. He's out looking for her now."

She decided to look at Cally now, clearly more confused by my presence than she wanted to admit. It frustrated me.

"It was something about her coming here early in the morning yesterday but she didn't stay for long."

"Did he not follow her? She can't get very far right now."

I tried to calm my nerves as I replied, but I wasn't prepared for feeling like this. It was as though my entire body was fighting the need to feel something.

"She wasn't alone. Liam had assumed she was with was

Alex." It all clicked as she spoke, finally realising that I was Alex. "But I can see it wasn't you. The police knew that though; I'm assuming you'd already spoken to them. Although I imagine they'll want to speak to you again."

She shot a look at me; half re-assuring, half wondering if I were as innocent as she thought; after all I was a stranger to her.

"What did they speak about?" Cally interjected.

"I don't know, although Liam did say she wasn't happy about it and left in a hurry."

My phone began buzzing against my leg.

"Mum? Anything?"

"Alexander, the police want to speak to you again." There was a fear in her voice, the kind of fear that comes with years of racial suppression. "Can you come now?"

"I'm coming."

Neither Cally nor I spoke on the journey back. I couldn't help wonder if she thought I was in some way mixed up in this. For a brief moment I knew what it felt like to be guilty before proven innocent. It became quickly clear how the impact of one person's accusation could shape the fate of a life. A simple sentence or passing remark can place you at a place where you had never before been. The most surreal part was how quickly other people jumped at the chance. The desperate need for a solution or a quick fix meant that any answer would be accepted if it made even the slightest bit of sense.

"Alexander, quickly, come inside." Mum was waiting for me outside the Herberts' house.

Mr Herbert smiled at me as I entered the house, placing one hand on my shoulder in reassurance.

"Alexander, please take a seat." The police officer gestured towards the sofa. There were two other officers standing in the corner, one holding a note pad and the other staring. The room was cold despite the evident stuffiness created by the heated building. The one standing officer sent a small smile towards me whilst the other barely looked up. I felt convicted.

"We just want to ask you a few questions," the police officer beside me said, sitting opposite me in the room. Mum sat next to me, her hand shaking as she gripped my fingers between her own. I was so uncomfortable with human contact but this felt more necessary for her, so I squeezed back in reassurance. I didn't reply to the officer; I couldn't speak.

"Could you tell us where you were yesterday morning at around seven?"

I couldn't help but dart my gaze to each officer individually, before cautiously wondering if this fidgetiness made me look guilty.

"I was home yesterday morning. I didn't go into school."

"Why were you not in school yesterday?" the officer replied. His look was soft but a tone of accusation placed in the back of his throat.

"I don't know, I was just feeling unwell." My answer was terrible and everyone knew it. It was a clear lie and I couldn't hide it. There is something about mental health that still holds a stigma. Had I just said to the officer I was feeling conflicted about my personalities and insecure about my existence in the world, he might've believed it more but I just couldn't say that.

The officer with the pad of paper paused to look up for the first time, scanning my face as if it would provide him with the evidence he needed.

"Was anyone home with you?"

"My mum was, before work." I looked at Mum who had

barely moved the entire time; she was staring straight at the officer, alerted to everything he said.

"What time was work?"

She remained stationary as she spoke, careful with her words.

"I left the house at eight and had spoken to Alexander just before this."

The officers exchanged looks.

"We're mostly interested in the hours between say six thirty onwards; can you be sure that your son was in the house before eight o'clock?"

I felt invisible as they spoke.

"Of course he was," she replied with such conviction it was impossible for the officer to press further.

"Okay, thank you both," he finished. I was ready to sigh in relief but he interrupted me before I could. "Oh, one more thing, I need the details of your car please: colour, make, model and registration. And stay local."

"Are you okay, son?" Mr Herbert asked, joining me on the front step as mum provided the officers with the requested information. I couldn't speak, so I nodded at him cautiously. "I'm sorry you had to do that."

He sounded sincere and for the first time in the past thirty minutes I truly believed at least one person didn't doubt me.

ROMOLA

We spent the rest of the morning hunting for a phone charger in the house. Jake's parents hadn't installed a landline due to the access to mobiles and part of me wasn't ready to call home yet either. Neither of us had any battery left on our phones.

"What do you want to do?" Jake asked, leaning back against the sofa arm so that he could look directly at me. He was so forward with everything; it was an unfamiliar confidence that I didn't expect him to have. His appearance was so edgy and nervous, I had imagined him insecure. It was invigorating. I felt alive around him.

"One more day. I doubt they've even noticed me yet."

My stomach gargled as I spoke. It had gotten progressively worse throughout the day, finding itself in a new state of pain. I was frequenting the bathroom to hide the heaving impulses as my stomach tried to release the knots. My demon was transcendent.

"Are you sure?" he laughed as he spoke. It was slightly mischievous and made me feel restless.

"Yes."

I had curled my legs up against the back sofa cushions, pressing them in gently to avoid our legs intermingling. Jake was less cautious, brushing his against mine occasionally in a playful menace. I couldn't help but compare it to the timid tension between myself and Lex when we nervously brushed hands in his car. I felt confident with Jake in a way that I couldn't predict. It was either perfect or dangerous. Either way, it was real.

"What shall we do now?" he teased, his voice calmed by the cannabis and his manner slowed. It was almost as though everything was considered, each move he made felt calculated.

"Anything and nothing," I replied innocently.

He leant in towards me and my stomach started pounding. I didn't know what I thought of Jake. He was here and kind to me. He was confident, carefree and made me feel okay to be myself. But he wasn't Lex.

"Pizza and a film?" He laughed, pulling away just as his body almost collided with mine. It was teasing and made me curious of what I had missed. My body felt slightly defeated, as though it had prepared for something but not fulfilled.

"Sounds good," I replied,

I felt conflicted, rushing as quickly as I could to the bathroom before my stomach betrayed me.

The bathrooms in this house were almost more exquisite than the rooms. On the downstairs floor there were two large bathrooms and a smaller one to the back of the kitchen. Inside one was a long sofa, which I later learnt to be called a chaise longue, a fancy sofa for stretching yourself across comfortably. It seemed ridiculous to have one in a bathroom, but so much of this house didn't make sense. It was unfathomable that there was only ever a family of three here when they visited, whilst there were so many vacant bedrooms.

I stared at my reflection in the mirror, wiping my mouth for the thousandth time, desperate to confirm there was no excess vomit. I brushed my teeth quickly, before storing the brush and paste away. I could feel the tears building behind my throat before they poured. The strange thing about tears like these is how they never seem to end. Homesickness had found its way into my mind; it was fuelled by a quick realisation of guilt.

Staring at the person in front of me, I didn't recognise her. It felt like I had created a new personality, layered over myself. I began rubbing intensely at the skin beneath my eyes, desperate to wash away some of the staining mascara. I looked like a celebrity mid breakdown, minus the cosmetically induced beauty plumping. My puffy face look was a direct result of sobbing.

I splashed my face again, this time benefitting from the coldness, as my eyes had finally stopped fighting it with the tears. I lay down against the chaise longue and just breathed.

The melancholy left me heated with a burning stomach and pulsing heart. I waited for it to subside but it refused, turning instead into a vicious anger. I could no longer stay laid down. The girl who sobbed at the sink infuriated everything inside me. She was weak and hollow, controlled by her anxiety. I refused to be her now.

My chest shot up, followed less quickly but with equal enthusiasm by my legs. In my mind this was powerful, energised and smooth, when in fact I stumbled less heroically out of the bathroom. I didn't know what was happening, all I knew was that my stomach didn't fuel me; it was a new kind of energy fuelled by frustration. Jake was back on the sofa, scanning through Netflix. He looked great; his hair was down, caressing his cheek again. He smiled a little when I sat back down, but barely lifted up from scanning the TV. I watched him for a while, cautiously waiting for my fears to nudge me out of this. But they didn't.

"Jake," I began.

He looked up but before he could reply I kissed him.

A little startled, he held back, his motions calm and resistant. I pulled away quickly.

"Do you not want to?" I snapped, quickly offended that I had misread all his unsubtle hints.

"NO, I do. Of course, I do, but we don't have to."

A single pang of anxiety shot through my stomach, soon conquered by my energy.

"I want to."

This time he didn't resist, leaning back into me so that we pressed against the sofa arms. His kiss was gentle much like his mannerism but unexpectedly firm and it felt like the control was always with me. Encouraged by his tenderness I felt excited, pulling him closer to me until his body was directly over mine. I couldn't help but imagine how much more comfortable this might've been on the chaise longue. Sniggering a little but continuing to trace his body with my fingers, I followed the curves of his back, pausing occasionally to pull the hold in closer. His body was lean and strong, so different to Lex.

"Shall we stop?" Jake asked, pulling away at my hesitation.

"No," I snapped, pulling him closer to me, but all I could think about was Lex. With each movement of our lips I pictured Lex's beautifully big lips that would spread into a teasing smile every time he saw me. Each section of body that my fingers touched I would imagine the strong curves of Lex's arms or the way our fingers would lock and it felt like they were wrapped endlessly together. I could feel Jake's hand begin to climb up my shirt.

"Wait," I blurted, pulling myself up to sitting. "I'm sorry, I think you were right. We should stop."

He looked confused, lifting himself completely away from me to the other side of the sofa.

"Of course." He smiled his carefree grin. "It was fun though."

I relaxed back into the sofa, laughing at his ease of everything. Just then the doorbell rang.

"That will be the pizza."

Jake shot up to collect the pizza. Grabbing a cushion, I pulled it tight into my stomach. It was in that moment I realised that I was homesick for Lex, but I still wasn't ready to forget what he had done.

ALEXANDER

There was no further word from the police for the rest of the afternoon. I felt like I was waiting for a verdict to come in. Having spent years avoiding conflict, appeasing the status quo and conforming to what others wanted of me, it felt peculiar to be here, accused for just existing.

I had driven to every place she might've gone about five times before the phone call. Eventually I found myself parked at the bottom of Crow Hill, just staring hopelessly out of the window. At first, I didn't flinch when the phone rang. It took a while to register it as being in the car.

"Hello," I mumbled, but the sound was silent, muffled by a gentle background noise. I looked down at my phone but I didn't recognise the number.

"Rome, is that you?"

I could hear her breathing but she didn't speak.

"Are you okay? Where are you?"

"I'm okay, Lex."

Her voice sounded calm.

"Romola, you need to come back, everything is chaos here without you."

"I will, soon. I just needed to let you know I'm okay. I don't have my phone right now."

"Where are you?"

"I'm safe, Lex."

She went silent. I couldn't find the right words to say.

"Romola, your parents are going mad here, they're worried sick."

She didn't speak, she just sighed.

"I'll see you soon," she replied before hanging up the phone.

"Rome? Romola?" But she had gone.

I tried quickly to call her back but the phone had been turned off.

I chucked my phone at the passenger seat, brushing my hands across my face in disbelief. It was so against her character I couldn't quite believe it. It took a minute before I realised the situation I was in, having to now take this information to the police.

On the journey back I traced over my past confrontations with the police. The first being at twelve years old when I was unjustly stopped in a department store where they searched my bag without reason. Second was at fourteen, when a police officer decided to do a random drugs search, choosing to only check the two black guys in our group before concluding that we were clean – in a group of eight.

I wasn't nervous to be confronted by them, just cautious of the outcome.

Entering the Herberts' house, the vibe was completely different to before. The police who had once watched me enter the room, barely looked up as I approached. Something had changed here.

"What's happening?" I asked Mum as I entered the kitchen. The Herberts' faces were panic-stricken.

"You're in the clear at least, the police have located a car leaving Crow Hill around the time Romola left Beanies and have followed it out of town. They've had to broaden the search because they'd anticipated it to remain local. No one ever thought she would've left town."

I was startled at the information; it hadn't occurred to me that she was elsewhere when she'd called.

"Mum, I just spoke to Romola. I was coming here to pass on the information."

Mr Herbert shot up, pulling his hand off his wife's shoulder, alerted by my remark.

"What's that, Son?"

He looked so confused, for the first time he was staring at me in disbelief.

"She called me about fifteen minutes ago on a number I couldn't recognise. I tried calling her back but the phone must be off. She wanted to tell me she was okay and safe."

The news didn't appear to be of much comfort to Mr Herbert. He looked like everything had finally hit.

"She's okay," he repeated. "She's okay?"

His question was rhetorical, said in a sigh of disbelief. As I watched him begin to pace around the room, it was clear that he wasn't processing the information correctly. He was trapped between the concern of a father and the hint of betrayal at his daughter refusing to come home.

"You must tell the officer in charge, Alexander," Mum nudged to me after a few minutes of silence.

The officer was reluctant to give me a moment of his time.

"Can this wait?" he kept repeating as I started to talk, refusing to look up from his research.

"It's Romola. I've had contact with her."

Within a second everyone stopped working; their untrusting glares resumed. It was as though my pardon had been lifted and their original prejudice confirmed. When I eventually relayed the entire conversation, the room divided. There were a few that returned to their work, absorbing the new information to apply to their case. They asked me for the mobile number and began tracking the owner history. Others were less forgiving, staring at me hard to see if I caved. These were the ones who deep down felt that I was guilty.

"I've got it," shouted an officer sat in the corner of the room, face into a computer. She began waving her hands towards the inspector.

"Name?"

"Jake Guildford."

Everyone looked at me, waiting for me to elaborate; but he was a stranger.

"He's a student at your school, Alexander. Do you know him?"

"Not at all."

"He's new to the school," Mum interrupted, trying to diffuse the evident frustration in the room.

"We need all the information you can gather on Jake Guildford, okay?"

The officer at the computer nodded, pushing her head back into her laptop.

Within minutes they had located his parents, called them and taken details of any relevant places he might've taken her. The officers set out a plan and each headed off to different locations. The previously bustling house was vacant, with just Mum, the Herberts and myself sat staring in disbelief.

"Do we just wait?" I felt helpless and angry.

"Do you know who Jake is?" I asked Cally as we sat on the steps to the house waiting for information.

"I know who he is, but I don't know him. In fact, he might be one of the only people I don't really know. He's one of those mysterious types who stick to themselves."

"Is he okay?"

"I mean, he smokes far too much weed if that counts as okay." She laughed a little as she spoke, immediately collecting herself. "But I really don't know anything about his character or that Romola even knew him."

"Does she?" I asked. "It's pretty against her character to leave like this."

"True, but even more against her character to leave with someone she doesn't know."

Everything felt mellow. I had counted on the fact that I was the allusive one and that Romola was unchanged.

"I can't just wait here."

"But the officers said we should, right?"

"Well, I can't. Where would they go, his house here, in the city or by the coast?"

As I said it aloud I realised just how wealthy this Jake must be. A pang of jealousy shot through my body.

"The coast?"

ROMOLA

I hung up the phone to Lex, thinking it would've left me comforted to hear his voice, but it left me feeling stupid. I turned off the phone and chucked it back under the pillow next to Jake's seat. As I watched Jake heading back into the room, my breathing sped up. He placed the pizzas in front of us on a coffee table and grabbed us both a slice. It was a small detail that I couldn't shift from my mind. One of those significant clues that send your entire world into confusion. My stomach rippled back into an acidic burn of warning. This time my anxiety was warranted, as everything began to shake.

"Are you okay?" he asked. A concerned look spread across his face that I struggled to believe. He handed me a slice of pizza, which I took with a steady hand.

"I'm fine," I snapped, biting on the pizza I had no stomach for.

Jake had battery, three bars of battery and must've had it the entire time.

This time it felt different. When his legs spread out across the sofa, touching mine gently, they felt like a stranger's. When he tilted his head back carefree, it looked like mockery of my situation. In one moment, everything seemed to be shaking.

"Shall we watch something else? Or do something else?" he asked as the movie ended. There was a crease below his eye that deepened as he smiled. I watched his face try to charm me again, but this time it felt cold. His expressions were those of a liar.

"Sure," I replied, carefully. "Let's watch something else."

He passed me another slice of pizza, having not realised I had barely touched mine.

"Series instead?"

I shrugged in agreement.

The sunlight slowly faded and the night began to howl. The once bright afternoon room, dulled into a cold large house. I tried desperately to absorb myself into the programmes. Tomorrow I would be returning home.

"Jake?" I began, deciding I needed to know what was happening.

He looked at me face on as though his drug-induced haze had finally lifted after devouring an entire pizza.

"What's up?" He looked kind, but I wouldn't be deceived this time.

"Jake, you had battery on your phone," I began. His face dropped slowly and he began shifting in his seat. "You lied?"

"Wait, Romola." He was uncomfortable and I wasn't used to seeing him like that. In fact, I wasn't used to seeing him like anything. I really barely knew him. "I can explain."

Just as he spoke there was a knock at the door.

"Who's that, Jake?" I asked, unable to keep the tone of my voice constant. I was afraid; truly afraid.

"I have no idea, Romola. I promise." He stood up and headed towards the door. "Wait for me to explain."

For the first time this large house was no longer magnificent. The rooms that I had stood in, awed by their grandeur, were now cold.

"Who is it?" I began as Jake headed back into the room. But he didn't speak. His face was ghostly.

"Um," he began, but he didn't need to continue. Following

behind him were two police officers.

"Miss Herbert?" one of the officers asked, heading straight towards me.

"Yes."

"Could you both please come with us?" he said rhetorically. "Your parents have been searching for you."

Heat filled my face. I couldn't speak. I couldn't move.

"Romola, do you hear what I'm saying to you?" the officer repeated. "You need to come with us now. You too, Mr Guildford."

It startled me hearing his last name. I finally realised just what I had done. I had left home, with no contact to anyone, with someone whose last name I didn't know.

I nodded, following the officers out of the house, limping defeated.

ALEXANDER

By the time we reached the motorway she had been found and was heading back with the police. We drove a little longer, before turning around and heading back to the Herberts' house. News of her safety had changed the vibe. An anxious father was pacing around the previously silent space and Mrs Herbert was chatting with my mum in the kitchen over a cup of tea. It was the sign of hope and relief.

It was past midnight when two headlights shone through the window of the living room. Everything stopped. The conversation muted and no one moved.

"Is she here?" Mrs Herbert finally said, when the car had been turned off and lights disappeared. There was silence except for the distant sound of footsteps tracing up the path. Romola's parents both sped to the door in anticipation.

"Romola," her mum called, running towards her as she entered the house. She didn't speak; she just let her mum embrace her. I waited for her to look up, to see me there and do something. Anything. But she didn't, she just stood allowing her parents to talk at her and hug her.

"We've spoken to her a little and it seems okay. There will be no charges placed over Mr Guildford as Romola has re-assured us the journey was consented to. He will be taken to his parents this evening. She does appear to be shaken, but we will leave her with you now, so that no more police time is taken up." The officer was clearly annoyed.

"An officer will call by tomorrow to follow up."

"Okay, thank you." Michael Herbert shook the officer's hand. "Thank you so much."

One nod and the officers had gone. The busy headlights shot up and the house was silent again.

"Alexander, let's head off," Mum said, gesturing towards me.

I waited for my name to nudge her to look up, but Romola didn't move. She stood, staring at the floor, motionless.

"Cally, we'll drop you home."

Romola shifted a little as Mum spoke to Cally, but didn't look up.

As we left the Herberts' house everything was different. The same house I had spent so many carefree days in now looked worn. The house was shelter to a broken family. It was a familiar darkness that spread over the home, but this time the darkness wasn't mine.

The following day I was reluctant to go into school, but Mum was insistent. It was past two in the morning when we finally went to sleep. She chose the moment we got home to address the events with me.

"Did you know anything that was going on with her, Alexander?"

"No."

"I can hardly believe that, after the time you've spent together recently."

She was looking at me in a new way; her brow was dipped low and raised at the edges.

"I mean, I knew something about Sarah and Michael, but I only found that out the other day."

Her face spread wide in surprise.

"What does that mean?"

I felt too tired to delve into the events at school, but I knew she wouldn't let the conversation end until I did.

"Sarah has been having an affair."

Mum looked uncomfortable, her shoulders shifting, and she pressed her fingertips into her forehead.

"Yes, I've heard. It's a complicated situation."

"Not for Romola," I scoffed under my breath.

"No, you are right," Mum replied, clearly ignoring the volume of my reply. "So she knows then?"

I stared at Mum in disbelief for a moment.

"Mum, everyone knows. It was printed on paper and shared all over the school. Mrs Herbert's affair was with BWC's head teacher."

This time it was Mum who was speechless. She turned around and walked into the kitchen to make a cup of tea. This was what she always did when things didn't make sense. When she argued with Dad, she would silently make her tea and stand staring at nothing. I would always imagine the way her thoughts moved, tracing in maps around her mind, silent from the outside but chaotic within.

"I'm just glad she's had you there to support her through this," Mum eventually said, "and this Mr Guildford... as wrong as her leaving was."

I didn't reply; I just left her there staring at nothing.

Jed called me over when I headed into school the next day.

"Catch you later, mate." I nodded, walking past everyone as I headed inside. I wasn't sure where she would be. I had never seen her at school to know where she hung out or if that would still be the case. It was only a few minutes before the bell would ring for class and I was desperate to find her.

"Is she here?" Cally asked me as I neared the lockers.

"I don't know. I haven't seen her."

Just as we spoke, Jake Guildford walked past us. He barely looked up, evidentially avoiding eye contact.

"Is she here?" I shouted at him, but he didn't look up.

"She's not coming in," he replied before disappearing behind a door.

I was infuriated that he knew more than me. After everything, she was still talking to him.

ROMOLA

The thing about humiliation is that it doesn't ease up the longer time goes on. If you don't face it, it just mulls there waiting for the optimum moment for its success. My humiliation might've disappeared a little after the events at school, maybe even after the awkward dancing in the Barn. Those humiliations might've eventually turned to pity and distant smiles from people at school. It might even have led to teasing or whispers. But the humiliation that was created from days of curiosity, and the rumours about my disappearance, was unfathomable.

Do you know she was kidnapped by Jake and locked in the basement of his parents' house? The police had to find her.

I heard he harassed her. He's such a creep.

Wasn't it that she was so desperate she begged him to take her, because her mum's a slut? I mean it sounds like the whole family is.

Did you hear that she faked her disappearance for attention? Such a brat.

These are just a few threads on my social media.

"The school agreed to let you return on Monday." Mum came

into my room the next day to tell me. She was being over friendly. Dad was the opposite; he couldn't look at me.

"Will he ever talk to me?" I asked as she sat on the end of my bed.

"If he'll talk to me, then I know he will talk to you soon," she replied, her head bowing as she spoke. "He's just hurt right now."

I still hadn't spoken to Mum about her affair. It was clear that she was desperate to open up the conversation. She was staring at me as though she was expecting me to run again. I felt guilt residing in my stomach as I watched her face shake as she tried to smile at me. Looking at her, I could see the young woman she once was; the person before me.

"Why did you do it?" I asked without meaning. There were sections of me that wanted to shout at her; that wanted to know everything about it. I shifted, waiting for her to respond; my room becoming smaller as we spoke.

"Honestly," she began, her eyes scanning my room, "things haven't been good with your dad for quite a few years. But whatever you think isn't what happened. It is what might've happened, but it didn't get that far."

I winced as she spoke, but I knew she was sincere.

"How could you do that to Dad?" I snapped at her, regretting it immediately.

She was silent for a while, staring at a pile of old books stacked on my desk.

"It was all much simpler then." She nodded towards the Jacqueline Wilson and Cathy Hopkins books that I'd spent my pre-teens devouring. "You still needed me and we were all a team."

"I just needed someone to talk to and your father couldn't be that. I was lonely."

I listened to her quietly; inside, my body was battling every emotion possible. I felt sick, fuelled by anger, but softened by a weird sense of understanding. I wasn't planning on letting her know this, I wanted her to know she was wrong but as I looked at her she was different. I had been so busy wrapped up in my life I hadn't seen her age. The face that always smiled at me, always prepared my dinner or asked how my day was, no longer looked the same. Beneath her eyes were deepened circles that travelled into gentle lines in the corners. Her eyes looked pale, like they had lost their pigment.

"It was just someone to talk to," she repeated, this time to herself.

We sat together for what felt like hours, silent, until she eventually got up to leave.

"Alexander called to speak to you this morning," she added before disappearing behind the door.

"How is the wedding planning going?" I asked. Liam called later that afternoon, he sounded cautious.

"I'm pretty sure Jen has a lot of it planned already." He laughed into the phone. "How are you?"

There was awkwardness in our conversation; I could tell he was calculating what to say. It was quickly clear to me that no aspect of my life would return to normal. This was one of those life-changing incidents that rippled its way into every section of your relationships, cementing the differences. Guilt was echoing in his voice, but I couldn't help but notice something extra there too. It wasn't clear and could easily be my paranoid anxiety taunting me, but it seemed almost certain that Liam was irritated.

"I'm fine," I snapped, attempting to close the pity party

before it began. My phone was full of messages. Aside from the ones that trickled in from school classmates trying to pry into the details of everything that happened to me, or the ones that merely messaged to tell me I was "clearly troubled", there were the ones full of pity. The majority of these were from Cally, family and even Lex. They were the absolute worst and filled my stomach with a deep sickness that felt permanent.

"Oh great," he replied with a bitter enthusiasm that made me certain he was holding onto something.

"How are you, Liam?" I spat back into the phone, built-up frustration peeling through my gritted teeth.

"I'm fine." He choked trying to squeeze the words out. "Just confused I guess."

I didn't reply. I was immaturely enjoying adding to his torment. It was because I knew where this conversation was going. Everyone wanted an explanation from me. Cally wanted to know why I did it, and if it was her fault. Lex wanted to know why I was with Jake. Liam wanted to know why I blew up at him before I left. With Liam I knew this kind of anger. It was the type that a sibling feels when things pace through fear of loss to anger. It was that unforgivable betrayal that can only be felt when you are found safe.

"Well, I'm glad you're fine." He scoffed, almost laughing as he spoke. "You're fine now. Great."

There was no disguising the sarcasm in his voice now, but I didn't know what he wanted from me. Nothing I said to him before I left was unwarranted.

"Liam, what do you want me to be? Would it be easier for you if I weren't okay?"

"At least that way I might be able to get over it."

"GET OVER WHAT?" I spat, rolling my eyes.

"The fact that you would run away like that just after arguing with me. Romola, I thought that was the last memory I would have of you."

I couldn't speak. We just stayed there, phones to our ears in silence. Nothing I'd say would be right.

Eventually he hung up.

It felt as though I were restricted to my room again, except this time it wasn't at the mercy of my broken body. This quarantine was voluntary hiding from the outside world. My demon was permanent, and darkness clouded every thought I had in doubt. I didn't want to move any more for fear that my next action could evoke a ripple of drama. I felt like a wrecking ball into everyone else's lives and the only intention was to demand some more attention onto mine. My selfish little stunt was enough to confirm that I could never put myself first, ever again.

ALEXANDER

Everything and nothing had changed.

"Alex, would you do a speech for us?" Rachel asked. "It would just be something short. This is obviously not a typical wedding."

I was still trying to get over the fact that my dad was getting married again.

"Uh, I guess."

It had been three months since they told me they were engaged, exactly three months and eleven days since I had last spoken to Romola. Everything and nothing had changed.

"Thanks, son," Dad said proudly, his hand gently resting on my shoulder. It didn't feel strange any more, he was much more affectionate now. But then, everything was easier now.

"Are you still okay to check out the band on the weekend too, Alexander?" Rachel smiled, topping up the coffee in my mug as she spoke. Dad's bachelor pad was no longer the slick, leathered, industrial building it had been four months ago, but the coffee was consistent.

"Yeah, it's no problem. Just send me the address."

"Maybe you could take your friend with you?"

Dad glared at her as she spoke, shaking his head a little in warning. Rachel was sweet, had that genuine kindness about her that made her impossible to not like. I had tried for a while when things were becoming serious between them. This was when I was angry for Mum.

"Are you still not speaking with Romola?" she asked innocently, clearly not connecting the sharp hints from Dad as a topic to avoid.

"No."

"Maybe you could just ask her anyway."

"Rach, it's okay," he eventually cut in, shaking his head to discourage her continuing. "I'm sure Alex has other friends to go with. Thanks again, kid, it was a silly thing to double book next weekend."

I smiled to re-assure them, but my attention was elsewhere.

Leaning back into the carefully plumped velvet pillow beneath me, I lost myself in the thoughts of what might've been had Romola never gone away that weekend. My life had taken a sharp turn since. Everything was good, except Romola.

ROMOLA

I knew I was supposed to be somewhere. That feeling sat at the back of my mind, nudging me towards something, but I couldn't find it. Everything was different now, everything and nothing. My demon was now permanently dictating my every action, finding concern in every possible outcome. I found myself obsessing over whether to brush my teeth or wash my face first. The confusion left me staring at my reflection in the mirror for an additional five minutes before I retreated to breakfast without doing either of the tasks. Everything had changed and nothing.

"Will you be staying at your dad's this evening?" Mum asked me over breakfast. She was watching me closely, as if trying to determine which task I had decided on.

"Uh, yeah, I think so."

Dad had moved out two weeks after I returned from the coast. He started talking to me a week after, but the conversation was small. The move was originally temporary. He had said it was to give him thinking space, but neither Mum nor I thought he would return. That 'space' seemed to feel more permanent with every extension of the short-term let.

Mum was watching me more now. It had become her new pastime; the thing that kept her busy between work, enough to distract herself from the empty space in her bed. I officially had all the attention I had ever wanted on me, but now I no longer wanted it. The worst part of everything was how everyone told me none of this was my fault. Things were apparently bad between them before; which was evident with the arguments and blatant affair. Yet I couldn't help but connect the truths. Before I left, they were still together; we were still together. Now we ate breakfast alone in a hollow house. Now I did everything alone. But I preferred it that way because the consequences of my actions were more contained. That way my demon wouldn't have to worry so much.

"Okay, well tomorrow I have someone I'd like to you to meet."

My stomach rippled acid into every section until my limbs shook.

It was too soon for her to have someone new and yet part of me – the cynical part – didn't dismiss the thought. We had put the affair aside, like an out-of-date food pushed further to the back of the cupboard, only to ferment more.

"Tomorrow, I can't," I shot back at her, my words hard enough that I bit down on my lip, piercing enough for blood to taste onto my tongue.

"It's a someone I knew years ago. A distant friend," she began, tilting her head to the side like she always does when she has something difficult to say. My mind trailed off into visions of Mum rekindling a lost love.

"He specialises in counseling for youths," she finally added.

My teeth neglected pressing into my lips long enough for my mouth to part in shock.

"Mum, I'm… " I was about to say fine, when heat shot through my stomach stopping me.

"Romola, this one isn't optional."

I didn't argue with her. I didn't speak at all.

I was expecting her to take me to an office, where everyone

would see me enter and know exactly why I was there. I had already mapped that out in my mind, but this was different. The building was a tall town house with merely a small sign beside the door: Dr Abara, Counseling Services for Children and Young People. For the first time since Mum telling me we would come here, I felt my body relax. No one would recognise this house from the next. No one would know why I was here.

"Hi. We have an appointment with Dr Abara at eleven," Mum said politely to the receptionist as we entered the small waiting area. It was calm, with sparse walls and green plants filling into the corners and tables. There were only two chairs in the space, positioned at a short distance from the receptionist's table. She welcomed us and gestured to the seats for us to wait.

"Romola Herbert? I will let him know you have arrived," she replied as we sat down.

"Yes, great, thank you."

Mum reached towards a small coffee table laden with hardcover art books, a water jug and glasses. She poured us both a glass, drinking hers quickly. I watched her for a moment, her eyes flickering around nervously. It was strange to see her like this, more anxious than I was.

"Dr Abara is ready to meet you now, Romola." The receptionist smiled, gesturing me to follow her into the adjoining room.

"Take your water with you, Romola," Mum pleaded, unable to control her nerves now.

Dr Abara was a tall, slim, black man, dressed head to toe in shades of brown apart from a beige roll-neck top that popped through beneath his jacket.

"Romola. Welcome. I am Dr James Abara, address me

however you feel comfortable."

I nodded in response, unsure what to do.

"Please take a seat." He pointed towards the chair closest to me, immediately eliminating the decision of where to sit.

He had a buoyance about his character that made it hard to believe that he knew my mum at all. It was as though she had aged and he'd remained young. His room was similar to the waiting area, carefully crowded with green plants and small gestures to Africa. The back of the room was a carefully organised bookshelf that covered the entire wall; small wooden figures and carvings buried themselves between the books.

"How are you today?" he asked, sitting down opposite me.

Between our seats was a wooden coffee table offering water. I rapidly gulped down my filled glass and poured another, desperate to delay the conversation. He waited, patiently.

"Don't you need a note pad?" I asked eventually, avoiding his question.

"That's a good point. But that's not quite how I approach these sessions," he began. "Let's keep it simple today. I'm just going to chat with you."

"Oh, okay."

"Are you ready to talk to me?"

"I'm fine today," I replied to his initial question, now avoiding his latest. "It's not that I don't feel comfortable talking to you. It's just that I don't know what to say or how to start. It all just feels so ridiculous."

"I get that. But let's just have a go and see what happens." He smiled this time, a small, reassuring smile. "Tell me what happened to bring you in to see me today."

"It all began with an accident that left me trapped in my room for weeks."

As I started speaking, everything was broken, as though I was attempting to join together the pieces of a difficult puzzle. I pointed out the main events hoping that would be enough to avoid delving into each section. I didn't mind talking about any of it; I just wasn't ready to cry. I hadn't cried since Dad left.

"Tell me a bit more about the accident with the rugby player," Dr Abara asked once I'd finished my list of events.

"There isn't really much more to say. It just happened."

"Take me through it," he encouraged.

I hadn't thought back to that moment since then, it had all happened so fast and the focus was placed on the aftermath. Until now I had almost forgotten that the accident was an event in itself.

"I mean, it all began in the canteen."

As I began retracing my steps through the canteen, I could picture myself there exactly as I had been. I wasn't sure if it was Dr Abara allowing me to delve so deep into the moment that it felt so real, or the fact that I had done the same motions daily for four years of my life; following Cally.

"I was looking down at my pad of paper when he came running towards me. I could hear him coming, but it was too fast. Or, at least, I didn't expect him to come to me."

"Why didn't you look up?" Dr Abara asked when I paused. I had almost forgotten he was there, as I wrapped myself in the memory.

"I was too busy reading my work to Cally. It was my article for the school paper." I paused for a moment, tracing over the moment again and again in my mind. This time Dr Abara stayed silent.

"No, that wasn't it. I was always looking down in the

canteen. It's one of those places where everyone watches as you enter. In fact, Cally wasn't even listening."

"I understand."

I looked up at Dr Abara expecting him to say something, but he remained listening, waiting for me to elaborate further.

"Cally was never really listening at school. At home, we could talk for hours about everything. But at school, I was just talking at her. I think I had gotten so used to that."

"What happened next?" he asked.

"That was when he rushed into me and pushed me against the railing. I mean, not intentionally. He was reaching for the ball and fell on me. It was quick and I can't really remember past there. I think that's when I blacked out."

"Thank you for telling me. We're going to finish here for today, but I'd like it if you would come back this week. Can you do that?"

I nodded, placing my glass on the table as I collected my things to leave.

"Dr Abara," I began, as he waited for me to stand first. "I knew he was coming towards me."

"I see. Do you know why you didn't move?"

"I was afraid, to be seen."

"Thank you for telling me that."

"How was it?" Mum asked, rushing over to me as I headed into the waiting room.

"It was okay," I replied. "It was interesting."

I had intended on telling her it went well, but I hadn't expected to believe it. I hadn't expected any of it. As we left the building I found myself wanting to stay. In that room I felt like things would be okay. It wasn't like at home, where all the attention was on me – but as a 'problem'. I knew Mum meant well, but ever since getting back from the coast she would watch everything I did. The way she asked me questions either sounded pitiful or infuriated. All the attention I had desired was now mine, but it was loaded. With Dr Abara it felt professional, almost as though I wasn't dealing with myself at all, but the mechanics of the human mind. It was less patronising and more matter of fact. I felt normal.

ALEXANDER

The conversation with Rachel played over in my head. I found myself parked outside Romola's house, staring at the empty building. I was unwelcome here, but there was no car in the drive so I knew they were gone. On the front lawn I could still see us as children, sitting in the tree, Romola red-faced as I teased her. Even with innocent intentions I had found myself inflicting permanent disruption to her life. With that thought I was reminded of our last conversation together. Two days after she returned.

***

"Can I come in?" I asked, waiting outside her bedroom. The house was eerily quiet, as though no one had spoken for days. Perhaps it was the contrast to the frantic police-filled house I had visited a few days prior. But it felt darker.

"Lex, please can you go away."

"Rome, just let me talk to you."

She didn't answer, so I tried the door. As I entered her bedroom she barely lifted her head. Her eyes were transfixed to her ceiling; she looked vacant.

"Are you okay?" I regretted it as soon as I spoke, awaiting the fury that would prevail, but she was silent.

"Rome?"

She looked like a china doll, with her curly hair sprayed in a halo above her head. The room was tidy. The distant scent of disinfectant suggesting it was Mrs Herbert's work. An empty bucket sat beside her bed and a roll of toilet paper curled under her hand. It looked as though she hadn't moved for hours. I sat at the end of the bed waiting for her to speak but she didn't.

"I am sorry." As I spoke I could feel the weight sitting on my stomach. In a selfish way it felt good to finally admit responsibility for my actions. I had lived in two personalities for so long, it felt like a part of myself claiming its place. "Rome, I should've been there for you that day. I should never have left you alone to find out about your parents."

She winced, clenching her stomach with her fist as I spoke. With each word I spoke I could feel my burden lift, but her body tense. We had never spoken like this. I waited for her to reply. In my version of this, she would sit up marvelled by my self-discovery.

"Please just leave. You don't get it, do you?" she replied, turning over and curling herself into a ball.

"I want to understand."

We were both silent for a few minutes. I resisted the urge to lie next to her, still sitting upright at the end of the bed.

"Lex, I like you," she began. "No, I *liked* you."

As she corrected herself I could feel my entire body shift into a new alertness.

"I really liked you and you weren't there for me. WORSE." Her voice got louder, but crackled, as if it were taking her final bit of energy to push.

"I watched you with Alice that night at the barn. After everything that had happened to me, you were with her. You chose her."

"Rome." I began to speak but the reality of her words finally sunk in. I could feel him leaving. In this moment that should have been hers, I was watching him leave. Clarity returned as the desire to be someone else left my body. In this moment I was fully myself. The dislike I felt for who I had been left me motionless, watching my persona fade. I sat there drowned in the consequences of my actions.

"Just leave me alone. For the first time, I'm asking you to not hurt me any more."

Her words were like a final statement that couldn't be protested, if I could attempt to find a reason. I watched her for a minute; she was powerful in her self. Curled up in solitude, but in this moment undefeated. I stood up, taking one last look at her motionless on the edge of her bed, before leaving at her request.

ROMOLA

School was uneventful. I barely looked at anyone and they were careful to avoid me. At lunch I sat alone and everyone left it that way. Cally attempted to sit with me when I returned to school the Monday after, but gave up after three days of being ignored. I preferred it this way.

Everything felt lighter since visiting Dr Abara. For the first time in weeks I woke up without heavy acid lying in my stomach. I almost felt normal, until I thought of school. It was different now that I knew who I was before: cowering to avoid everyone. When you know something about yourself it is hard to not be anxious of it being obvious to everyone else, and anxious to not do it at all. I felt too good to bother with the trouble of school today. I couldn't truant; especially now that I was being watched like a hawk.

"You seem different today?" Mum said as we sat down to eat breakfast.

"I feel different. Can I walk today?"

I was grateful to be out of crutches, but it was the furthest I'd walked. Mum had been sure to drive me to school every day since I started back. She looked nervous to reply, clearly not excited at the new-found positivity. I knew she didn't fully trust me now and the idea that I could leave again was always at the back of her mind. She was also conscious that this change was directly after visiting Dr Abara and desperate to not undo any progress.

"Okay, then," she replied reluctantly. "Will you text me when you get to school?"

It felt patronising, but I knew I had inflicted in upon myself. "Sure."

"Romola?" The voice behind me was familiar but I couldn't place it. I had my headphones in so considered pretending not to hear.

"Is that you, Romola?" The voice was rushing behind, getting louder as it approached. I recognised the face from videos Lex had shown me. It was Daliah, a friend of his from his mum's church group. I knew so much about her and Jamal but we'd never met until now. I had no idea she knew me.

"Daliah?" I asked.

"You know me?" She seemed surprised.

"Yeah, I mean, I know of you. Lex told me about you and Jamal a couple of times."

"Haha, yeah he's a laugh. Wait… Lex?"

"Oh yeah, sorry, Alex."

She laughed, intrigued.

"There's got to be more to that name?"

It felt strange talking about him like this, almost as though nothing had happened.

"Yeah, it was a nickname he gave himself when we were kids."

"Sounds like Alex."

I couldn't help wonder how well she knew him.

"I haven't seen you walk this route. Will you be walking tomorrow too?"

We were approaching school now so I knew she'd want to scarper before being seen with me.

"Uh, probably," I snapped, keeping it short for her to leave.

"That's great. I find it so boring on my own. I'm such a morning person."

Something about that didn't surprise me at all. I smiled but didn't answer, giving her time to leave.

"Are you?"

She was super chatty – and not leaving.

"Yeah, I guess so. I mean I used to be."

"Great! Maybe tomorrow we could meet earlier and grab a coffee on the way in? If it's not too much of a diversion through town for you?"

We were in the school hallway now and everyone was looking at us, but Daliah didn't seem to notice. Or at least she didn't care.

"I'd love to get coffee tomorrow."

"Great! My form is up here." She pointed at the stairs we had stopped beside. "Catch you later, Ro?"

"See you later."

I had grown accustomed to disappointment. Setting out the following day at the newly discussed time, I had very little belief that Daliah would be waiting. The surprise planted itself across my cheeks in a wide smile, which my face had recently forgotten how to do. She was rushing along the path towards my house as I closed the front door. Her face was panting and her limbs weakening, making it clear that she had run far.

"I may be a morning person. But I always seem to be late." She laughed, as she came closer. "I mean, you don't get to look this good, without some effort." She gestured up and down her body as she spoke. I found myself in awe of her confident and nonchalant manner at her self-awareness. It wasn't cocky, but affirmative. After all, she looked amazing.

I laughed and nodded at her in a bashful response. There was something un-nerving in her confidence, like the positive self-evaluation was expected to be mutual. I wasn't comfortable with being closely observed. But it became quickly apparent that it was not Daliah's intention. She was far too free to put pressure where it wasn't wanted.

"So, how's school been since you got back?"

As she launched into the direct question it felt unloaded; in a similar way that Dr Abara had asked. It confused me for a moment and I wondered if she had missed the past few months and had no idea about what had happened. But her careful hesitancy quickly affirmed that she was aware and was simply asking the most avoided question.

"It's honestly been okay," I replied, with a surprising certainty. "Mostly people just leave me alone now."

"Most, but not me!" She laughed, nudging me in a way that made me feel immediately okay.

"Ha. You just wait," I joked. "You'll be running before you know it."

It felt great to laugh, but I secretly worried that she would take note of my comment and run.

In town we grabbed coffee and started heading to school. We chatted the entire way, her ease of character encouraging me to respond. As I watched this strange friendship evolve I felt momentarily thankful for the past few weeks. In this moment only, I felt like the events that had passed had led me to a character who I knew would allow me to just *be*.

ALEXANDER

When I left Romola's house three months before, I was filled with heavy regret and the clarity of knowing who I needed to be. In every aspect of my life I found it easier to just belong. Staring at the room of boxed belongings, it was finally time to move on.

"It's about time." Mum laughed from the doorway as I shuffled through boxes of the past, placing most of it into a box for charity.

"I guess so," I replied.

She sat beside me, flicking through old photos; most of which were Elle and me.

"Well that was an interesting pairing." She shrugged, rolling her eyes a little.

"What do you mean?" I asked, although I knew what she meant. There was something disheartening in knowing that she knew all along, who I really was. It took the crumble of Romola's life to prove to me that I was playing a losing game. Sometimes I wonder if I'd have realised it sooner, had Mum just shouted at me about something I had done. Any resistance might've caused me to snap out of it, but she always remained kind.

"Well, you know… she was into different things. I never really thought she got you."

I stayed quiet, wanting to bite back and ask her why she'd never said anything. But we didn't do confrontation.

"She was okay," I replied; Elle's character didn't deserve tarnishing. I was not the person Mum thought I was when we lived in the city.

She stood up, starting to leave.

"Would you be okay if I invited someone over this evening?" she nervously added.

"Sure. I'd like to meet him," I replied, knowing she was talking about a new boyfriend.

Things in her life had quickly improved since moving house. It was like watching the pressures of the city drop away and a new future take form. I couldn't help but parallel my life to Romola's. The consequences had been much greater for her, with the collapse of her family and school situation. I wanted to rush over there and comfort her. But since moving back here, I had managed to contribute to her downfall.

"Are you ready for exams?" Jed asked at lunch.

We had remained friends through all of it, but it was purely because of the history behind us. After my personality slipped further away from the douche personality I had lived with for the passing years, the guys fell back. We still had sports in common, so the general banter remained solid. The rest we left divided. At lunch I would often continue studying and they continued snarling at girls. I flicked my English Lit book closed and looked up at Jed who was handing me a coke bottle.

"As much as I can be," I replied seriously, but Jed laughed.

"With the amount you study, you better be, otherwise the rest of us are screwed."

I tilted the bottle to him in thanks for the drink and took a large swig until the bubbles fizzed into my head.

"I've had some catching up to do."

"With the move here, you mean?" he asked.

"Something like that."

I thought about all the years I had spent distracted.

"You coming away with History class this weekend?"

"Yeah. I plan to."

I was looking forward to getting away. I glanced over to the corner of the canteen where Romola sat with Daliah; they were laughing at something on a phone. I hadn't planned to go on the school History trip, until I saw that she was.

"Sick. The last bang before exams." Jed sniggered as his words attempted a rhyme.

"Is she coming?" Jed asked. My lack of response to his joke made it clear I was distracted.

"Who?"

"The person you watch every lunch," he teased. "Romola. Right?"

He looked sheepish, like he had discovered my biggest secret.

"I have no idea," I replied defensively, not wanting any unnecessary attention to be inflicted on her.

"You clearly like her though. You should ask."

He turned away as he spoke, finished with the conversation. I watched her again, as she nervously tucked her curls behind her ear, before they menacingly bounced back. I didn't know what I felt towards Romola. I knew she was important to me; she brought out the best of me in a selfish way. I knew that I missed her friendship and felt guilt-ridden for how she had been treated. I knew I watched her every day, wondering if she would look over. I knew that she had liked me, past tense. I had no idea how I felt about her.

ROMOLA

"Tell me how it feels?"

"It starts with a flick in the pit of my stomach. It's almost like a heartbeat building up and falling again so rapidly it feels as though I can't breathe. This is the warning. When I feel this I know it's coming and the thought makes it worse. Occasionally I can control it, pushing against the idea of being anxious and dismissing it as a fear. When this happens I can sometimes avoid feeling the rest of what is to come. If I don't, it's like a wave of acid that crashes against the inside of my stomach. It sits there long enough to burn before shooting up my chest to my throat. This is when I can no longer eat, no longer think and no longer see the future."

"Does it happen often?" Dr Abara asked.

"Before the last three months, it happened often, but with reason. It was social and sought only to ruin the progression of that aspect of my life. Now it's daily."

"Tell me more about it now."

"He's not constant, but when I wake my stomach is full of acid. When things surprise me, it bounces up my chest. Now it's just a fear, that nothing is certain and so no decision will be the right one."

"He?" he interrupted. "You said he?"

I had never admitted to anyone that I had given him a name. It was ridiculous now I thought of it.

"Um. My demon."

Dr Abara cleverly concealed his surprise. It was this that made it so easy to talk to him. It felt like there was no judgment.

"Just to clarify, you named the feeling of being anxious, 'your demon'?" he asked.

I nodded, avoiding eye contact as he spoke.

"Why do you think you did that?" He didn't sound patronising, not even curious. So I continued.

"Sometimes I felt lonely. Like this burden I was carrying had sectioned me off from everyone else. I was furious with it. It felt so real, but no one else could see it. So I named it for myself."

"So you made it more real?"

My face shot up, staring directly into Dr Abara's calm eyes.

"I mean. Maybe I did."

As I replied to his question the reality of what I had done sank in heavier than my demon ever had. The room felt warm, like everything was crashing around me at the realisation that I had chained myself to my anxiety. I could see it sat with me in the session, staring childlike at me wondering what this meant for us both. Neither of us knew how to part from each other, having lived so close together for so long. In my disappointment at being alone, I had filled it with the obsession of my demon. It wasn't that he didn't exist. It wasn't even that I wasn't anxious, but I had given him a form greater than an emotional reaction. I had given him humanity and control over my self.

Dr Abara stayed silent, allowing me to piece together the realisation that there were small aspects of my mental state that I was responsible for.

"Did I make it worse?" I asked, praying that he would have the answer I was desperate to hear.

He shifted in his seat, pouring me a glass of water.

"I can't tell you that. My job is to help you find the

conclusions for yourself. I think you know the answer to that question, it's been with you all along."

I found myself grinning at his carefully worded response. It was like a release of energy leaving as it pushed the smile into a gentle laugh, eventually finding myself caught in a burst of sweet laughter.

Dr Abara remained calm, allowing me to process the revelation without evaluation.

"What's happening?" he asked me.

"Nothing," I replied, with a gleeful bounce. "I can see what I have done and I feel different. Like there is something I can do to ease the pain. I can stop giving it so much life."

He nodded, reassuringly.

"That sounds good. Tell me more."

"Just by not letting it be too big. It's not that I think I won't be anxious. It just feels like it doesn't have to be so real now."

As I left Dr Abara's office, I didn't know what was to come. I didn't know if my positive realisation would stick or if it was just a blissful epiphany. But I didn't feel anxious about whether it would or not.

The following day was the History trip to London. Mum had told me I didn't have to go and every day prior to the last visit to Dr Abara I had considered not going. There were endless possible outcomes from the trip, both good and bad. The problem with exploring endings is it is much easier to conclude negative results. In my best picture I left the trip enlightened, and in my worst, I left the trip more broken and tormented than before. Now it felt okay, like the trip could be anything and I would handle it.

"Do you have everything you need?" Mum asked as we

climbed in the car. I was starting to worry that she was becoming more anxious than I was.

"I do. Besides, it's only two nights, Mum. We'll be okay."

I hadn't meant to say we, but she noticed it too. I meant her. She hadn't been alone in the house since before I was born. This was going to be strange for us both.

"Try to have fun." She smiled cautiously.

"You too." I laughed a little and we both smiled.

"Is it First Years too?" I asked Daliah, noticing Jed Jennings getting onto the bus. "I thought it would just be Year Elevens."

She shrugged her shoulders, flicking through her Spotify playlists.

"I think its Year Eleven and then First Year *'Formers'* History class too. That's what the form said, anyway," she replied, still staring at her phone.

The uncertain series of events was beginning to unfold and I had no idea what the outcome would be. I didn't panic, breathing deeply in and out to calm my body in anticipation.

"If it's First Year History then that means… "

"Alexander!" Daliah teased, punching the arm of the person stood behind us in the bus queue. The sweet smell of shea butter and sage filled my nose and sent gentle butterflies into my stomach. I could feel the space between us tightening my body. I couldn't move, focusing desperately on my breathing.

"Hey," he replied, sounding nervous.

I couldn't help wonder if he could feel it too, the heated tension that lay between us. This was the closest we had been in months, and it felt strangely exciting.

"See you on there," she joked with him.

I clenched my fingers together to wake up my body, praying

that he wouldn't sit near us on the bus.

"Here, Alex."

I hadn't told Daliah about Lex, we really hadn't spent long together. In fact, nothing really phased her so I doubt she would've considered it if I had. She was gesturing at the row beside us for him to sit in. I looked up and he was looking at me, clearly unsure whether to sit or not. Without meaning to I found myself smiling at him, just enough to be polite, but it was greeted by the warmest grin that lit up across his face. My stomach danced again and I knew that, as much as I tried to tell myself we were nothing, I still wanted more; I wanted Lex.

They chatted for about ten minutes before Daliah rested her head on my shoulder, passing me a headphone piece. It was something Cally and I would do, and for a moment I missed her too.

"Who are you sharing a room with?" Daliah asked. I sat up, rubbing my eyes as I realised we had arrived.

"Jed," Lex replied, gathering his bag to leave the bus.

"Okay. Well it'll be me and Romy if you wanna pop over later?" Daliah asked, clearly oblivious of the tension that shot me widely awake.

I could feel Lex looking at me again for a confirmation, but I couldn't look up.

"Maybe," he replied, a little disappointed. "We'll see."

"You better." Daliah laughed, linking her arm in mine as I stood up to get off the bus.

The hotel was basic, a Travelodge on the way into London. Some of the students were clearly disappointed, having anticipated fleeing to the city at night. I was excited, being away from home left me feeling energised.

"Are you and Alex okay?" Daliah asked as we chucked ourselves on the soft hotel beds.

"You don't know, then?" I replied, staring at the floral engraved pattern on the ceiling.

"Shit, no. What's up?"

"We haven't spoken for three months." I could hear her jaw open wide, in exaggerated disbelief.

"Fuck! I had no idea." She sat up. "Did I make that super awkward?"

"No. It was good actually. It felt normal."

"Shit. Romola. I'm such an idiot."

"HA! No, you're not." I laughed. "Besides it's been so long now. I'm not sure how I feel."

"And I invited him here tonight!"

"It's okay."

"No, I'll cancel it. Some others are having a meet-up in their room anyway. Let's go eat and then get ready to go there?"

I nodded.

The teachers were strangely distant since we got into the hotel. In a polite, English manner they had warned us against mingling, fraternising with the opposite sex and noise levels. It felt like the entire hotel was full of students and the requested noise levels seemed more for the sanity of the teachers.

"What are you wearing?" Daliah asked as we rummaged through our suitcases. I had only packed semi-casual clothes for the day. Naïvely I hadn't anticipated socialising at night, nor had I wanted to until now.

"Jeans and a t-shirt."

"More like something from me." She laughed, chucking me a little black dress.

"I can't wear this!" I laughed. "It's too… "

"Perfect."

There was very little arguing with Daliah. She was a level of pushy that gave you the confidence to do things but knew when to let you breathe. I could be equally snappy with her and with a little eye raise she'd be proud of my objection. Everything about her was liberated and wanted the same for those around her. She would make the perfect activist.

"I don't look too bad." I laughed, spinning to look at my reflection in the mirror. The dress had a deep plunge that glided around my flat chest and enough flare to bounce over my skinny body.

"You look hot!" She grinned. "Now let me do your hair."

She pulled out a bag full of hair products.

"Aren't they for Afro hair?" I replied ignorantly.

"Yeah, but, girl, your curls need some serious conditioning."

I looked at the mop of hair on the top of my head, which looked effortlessly good in the messy bun kind of way.

"Let me show you."

She began spraying my hair with water before pulling a thick shea butter mousse through the curls. I watched them bounce back up with an energetic shine that they never had before.

"That's incredible," I said as blonde curls sat in ringlets around my head. "I look so different."

"You look amazing."

Daliah slipped into a tight camo dress and wrapped a silk camo headband around the front of her braids. She drew a thick layer of eyeliner above her eyes, before matching the look on me.

"How can you do all this?" I asked, watching her in amazement.

"My mum taught me most of it to be honest and then YouTube."

"I wish my mum had taught me make up!" I replied. "You're so good."

"Well, you know me. I don't do things in halves."

We both burst out laughing. There was nothing 'half' about Daliah.

The room was already full of students. I had already checked to see that Alice wouldn't be on this trip. I planned most things to avoid her; like the timings I would use the toilets at school. I couldn't see Cally either; I hadn't really seen her since coming back to school. I wasn't purposely avoiding her, but we just stopped passing each other in the corridors and had no classes together. It was almost as though she had disappeared.

"I'll be one second, Romy, unless you wanna come?" Daliah said, rushing towards a girl who had been beckoning her over since we arrived.

"You go. I'm going to hold back a moment," I replied, staring at the crowded room, unsure how to approach the event.

"Do you want a drink?" A familiar voice from behind me sent the room spinning momentarily. I turned around slowly, taking in every inch of the person who stood before me.

"You're not wearing black?" were the only words I could say.

ALEXANDER

I could tell it was Romola by the way her body leant to the side, with one leg crossed over the other. She looked different, somehow. Always dressed in tracksuits or large t-shirts, she was wearing a black dress that fit tightly at the waist.

"You never miss anything do you?" I joked.

"I guess not."

"Is it my colour?" I asked lightly, trying to conceal my nervousness. I didn't know if she wanted me there.

"It suits you." She smiled. "It's green!"

"You look beautiful," I blurted, unable to contain myself. I felt instantly stupid, having already decided to not be too intense with her. "You are beautiful."

My thoughts were rolling out faster that my mind could object.

"Thank you," she replied bashfully. Her face turned scarlet and I felt terrible again. It seemed like I was destined to cause her embarrassment. But she was smiling.

"Where's that drink then?" she asked.

For a moment everything felt normal again.

"Let me get you one." I smiled at her, unable to keep my mouth still. "Will you wait for me?"

It felt unfamiliar; this newly found anxiousness. I could no longer flip onto another version of myself to hide behind, nor did I want to. Now it was different though; if she didn't like me now, it was 'me' she didn't like.

I grabbed two beers from the table before heading back to her. I was desperate to be fast, I didn't want her to leave.

"What was that band called, Alex?" Jed began to ask as I turned away from the table. I stared at him confused; my eyes darting back to Romola.

"Um. The National."

"Sick, yeah!" he replied, turning back to converse with Luke.

Relieved, I started heading back towards Romola but she was no longer alone.

"Alex," Daliah called as I approached them both. "Come, there's someone over here who wants to meet you."

She winked at Romola, thinking I hadn't seen, before pulling my arm towards a group at the far side of the room. I felt confused, wondering if Romola had asked her to direct me elsewhere.

"I'm sorry," Romola mouthed quietly.

For the next few minutes I found myself caught in a conversation that was impossible to leave. I tried desperately to close the communication but Daliah kept asking questions to include me in the conversation. Glancing over at Romola hopelessly, she looked mischievous. It was almost as though she was enjoying watching me squirm.

Her sheepish grin became uncontrollable as she laughed at my pain. She was beautiful when she smiled. It was one of those timid smiles that showed no teeth but consumed her face.

"Was it like that at your previous school, Alex?" Daliah's question pulled me away from the playful game of eye glances and face expressions I had begun with Romola.

"Uh. Sorry, I missed that one," I replied, trying to look interested in the comments directed at me.

"Alex, you're being requested in the hallway." A soft voice spoke behind me. I turned around to see a brunette girl with glasses grinning at me. I had never seen her before, but she looked surprisingly excited to speak to me. The conversation behind me moved on and I was quickly freed from obligation.

"Really? Do you know why?" I asked, desperate to not be dragged into another conversation.

"No, sorry, I don't," the girl replied, before turning to leave.

I glanced over to Romola, but she had gone.

As instructed, I left the hotel room and headed into the hallway. It was silent and empty but for a small figure sat against the wall at one end.

"Miss Herbert," I joked, addressing her as though nothing had happened between us. The familiarity made us both nervous.

"Hey."

"You saved me?" I asked. "How did you manage that?"

I slid down next to her, pressing my back against the cold wall to calm my nerves.

"I traded a message for the beer you gave me. It's amazing what people will do for a free drink." She laughed. "Although I'm pretty sure having a reason to talk to you sealed the deal."

"You're quite the secret agent."

"Now you know how I really got my leg injury," she joked.

There was a calmness about her that unsettled me. It was strange to feel our roles reversed.

"How is that?" I asked. I was desperate to ask more, to know how she was, but it was too soon for that.

"Good. Much better."

"That's great."

Awkwardness sat between us, filling the room with

thickened silence. It was almost as though our breaths danced in front of us, each new exhale pushing them further away but filling the air with heat. I listened to hers get louder and louder, met eventually by the deep moving of her heartbeat.

I wanted to tell her again that I was sorry, but this was a new space in time and there was no room for the past. I remained speechless, racing my breath with hers. I turned to look at her; she was staring straight ahead avoiding my eyes. Her lips began to curl at the edges. She turned to look at me as I moved in to guide a stray curl back behind her ear. There was so much unsaid in our glance. Meeting her eyes with mine, I felt the urge to tell her everything, from struggling with the fear of expectations to the reason I acted the way I did. In her eyes was understanding. I attempted to open my mouth, but nothing would find its way to my throat. I was lost in the moment with her.

Moments turned into minutes. Staring at her now felt like rediscovering a book and finally understanding everything. There was so much to her I hadn't seen or allowed myself to look at. I had a desperate urge to kiss her.

"Rome?" I began.

"Romola?" another voice echoed behind me, pulling us out of our trance.

"Cally." Romola nodded towards Cally. She began to sit up, using the wall to pull her from the floor.

"Romola, can we talk?" Cally asked, moving closer to her in a desperate attempt to close the space. "I really need to talk to you."

Romola looked down at me and I smiled wide at her.

"To be continued," I teased.

She nodded.

Moments later and I sat, my back pressed against the wall,

in the hallway of a Travelodge. For the first time in my life a few things felt certain. I had no idea where tomorrow would take me, but I knew that I was finally myself. I knew that what I felt for Romola was different to anything I had felt before. I knew that I didn't want to spend another day away from her.

ROMOLA

Watching my best friend sat at the end of my bed, bent over in tears, was unexplainably painful. A few months ago I had dreamt of this night. It was after realising how close Alice and Cally had been in those weeks prior to what happened. In that moment I wanted her to feel everything I had felt. I hadn't imagined ever feeling sadness for her again, but there was a darkness to her cry that sobbed of something much worse than the situation that was before us.

"What is it, Cally?" I asked, trying to stage my words between her sobs. It took her a few moments before she could speak, brushing her hair away from her face, as it moved through her tears matting together in a salty fur.

"Romola, I've messed up so bad with you and it's too much now."

A momentary pang of self-righteousness sat in my stomach as I watched her spill her apology to me. I knew she meant what she said, but it was typical Cally to still make the situation about her.

Watching her squirm in desperation for my affection I realised how different we were. I couldn't bear to see her in pain even for a moment.

"Cally, you were everything to me. More than what I felt for Lex, more than my parents who had always had their own life. You were the one who I spent every weekend with. It was you who I'd stay up chatting to over the phone, or could laugh with until my stomach hurt. It was you who broke me the most."

Her sobs became louder and her throat was dry as she began to cough between cries.

"I'm so sorry, Romy. I really am. Everything just got too hard. I couldn't please everyone any more and I thought if I pulled away from you, you would always be there. I took you for granted. But it went too far, and you got broken along the way."

As she spoke, rationality began to clear her tears. I passed her a tissue and pressed my palm against her shoulder.

"It didn't break me, Cally," I replied with so much certainty, I knew it to be true. "It would take much more than that to break me. But it hurt me more than you can ever know."

She bowed her head low again, like a child ashamed of their foolishness.

"But I'm okay now."

It was enough. She sat up and smiled at me in the proud way of a sibling.

"I can tell."

We spoke a little longer, but the conversation soon fell into general niceties. The thing about heartbreak, sometimes even when repaired, the pieces don't fall back into the same place. I wasn't sure if mine had room for Cally any more. As I watched her leave my room I felt contentment for the years we had spent together and thankful for the importance she played in these early years of my life. I knew this wasn't the end of our story, but it was different now.

The weeks that followed went by faster than the year that preceded. Lex and I were playing a lengthy game of 'catch me if you can', always stopping long enough to say hello and nothing more, before rushing into revision classes and eventually exams.

The free time I had outside of school I spent with Mum, re-doing the house in areas that she wanted help with. It was what she spent most of her time doing to avoid the hollowness of Dad's absence. There was little to no movement towards their reunion. There were of course the remarks from them both – "How's your mother holding up?" "Did your dad look well?" – but their stubbornness kept them both playing games. I had no idea when they would give up the fight, or if they ever would, but I didn't mind. They were clearly enjoying the new tension between each other, and I was more partial to that than the arguing.

Liam took a little longer to figure out. There was no apology letter or weeping at the foot of my bed. With Liam I needed to grovel.

"Is he here?" I asked Jan as I entered Beanies. It was my first day since finishing exams and it felt like summer had begun just in time. The sun sat high in the sky and brought with it a flurry of hikers that filled out the cafe.

"He's out the back, with Jenny."

I nodded to Jan who gave me a supportive thumbs up as I headed into the bakery. The warm buttery smell of fresh pastries filled the air around me, nudging my stomach into a heavy grumble.

"Romola!" Jenny grinned when she saw me enter. "I knew it was you by the grumbling stomach. Liam, get her a croissant."

"Thanks." I smiled as Jenny embraced me in the tightest hug.

"Here." She took the Pain au Chocolat out of Liam's reluctant hands and passed it to me insistently.

"I'll leave you two to sort this out." Jenny laughed, rolling her eyes towards me as she left.

She was always so chilled; it was the reason Liam and her

were so suited. He was the serious type, and she the opposite.

"This tastes amazing," I mumbled, attempting to soften the mood through crumbs of pastry. "You are so good at this."

He remained silent, kneading at a pile of dough that sat beside him on the floury surface.

"Jenny looks amazing. Wedding planning must be going well." I attempted to ease in with small talk, but he was unrelenting. "Look, Liam, I'm sorry. I get that it wasn't ideal me leaving after that argument."

"No, you really don't," he snapped.

"But you don't get how utterly alone I was at that moment."

He stared down at the bread beneath his palm, carefully avoiding my eyes.

"I know," he replied eventually. "Your mum says you're seeing someone?"

"She did?" I replied startled. "She told you?"

"Only me. I came over a couple of weeks ago to talk to you but you weren't in, she said you needed time." He looked up. "Shit, Romola, I fucked up. I should've been there for you."

"It's okay. It really is."

As I left Beanies it felt like everything was slowly falling into place again. I found myself wondering what would've happened had my life played out in any of the other scenarios my anxious mind had explored. There was so much calculation to those thoughts, it seems crazy to think that with that much focus on my future I couldn't physically manipulate the outcome. But that is life; a series of possible endings, influenced by decisions we make, unknowing of the future.

ALEXANDER

"You look beautiful," I said, watching her glide around the dance floor carelessly.

"I've still got the moves in me." She laughed, flicking the hem of her dress as she sped across the room. "Come on, show us your moves."

I was reluctant to dance, but watching her face fill with pride as she looked at me, I found it impossible to say no.

"Aha, that's my boy."

She looked young; her eyes glistened as she moved. I had seen this look in her eyes as a child, it was a look only for me, but it had faded over the past few years. We had always danced together, in the kitchen of the house. That changed as I grew up and her relationship with Dad fell away. Now, at his wedding to Rachel, she looked carefree.

"I learnt from the greatest." I grinned, mimicking her dancing.

"Did she come?" Mum asked, noticing my eyes flick around the room in search.

"I didn't see her at the church, but then it was a big ceremony." Rachel's small and simple wedding was three hundred people large.

"I'm sure she'll be here."

I had waited in the hallway of the hotel for her to return. I knew she wouldn't but found myself glued to the wall, unable to move on the chance that she did return. There was no way I was going to risk messing this up a second time.

"Did you find your seats?" Rachel asked. She had been watching Mum and I goof around on the dance floor for a little while, waiting for the appropriate time to come over.

"We didn't quite get that far." Mum laughed, eyeing up Dad's new bride. I had been surprised that Mum had been invited, and even more that she'd decided to attend.

"It's pretty busy, isn't it?" Rachel replied, a little embarrassed by her extravagance. "It turned out I wasn't the best wedding planner after all. It's difficult to know who to invite."

Her rosy complexion turned red.

"Obviously, you were both definitely invited," she added, attempting to retrace her steps.

Mum laughed a little too loud. I could tell she was enjoying watching Rachel squirm.

"Well, thank you. It's great to have somewhere to get dressed up for," she replied, as though it were a stranger's wedding and not the second wedding of her ex-husband. "Besides, it's about time we got to know each other. After all, you are my son's stepmother."

Rachel's jaw dropped as the realisation of her new role sunk heavily beneath her dress. Mum's laugh now turned into a howl and I joined her. She was magnificent in her newly liberated disposition. It took a moment but Rachel joined in, clearly taking note that the comment was less serious than she anticipated.

"I like you, Rachel, I think we are going to be a great family."

This time she relaxed, linking the arm Mum offered to her and following her towards the table plan.

As I watched them walk away, with a gentle nod towards Dad who was beaming wide at the scene, I felt overwhelmed with joy. I followed my thoughts back to the years that preceded and how heavy life had felt. The idea that my parents could get along had been a pipe dream in a reality of endless arguments and lengthy silences. Having spent months feeling alone, with a figurative family that barely spoke, I could see the possibilities in my future beginning to unveil. So long as I just continued to be myself.

As the room began to pour into the tables provided, I followed Mum's path to find my seat. The room was full of unfamiliar faces at an event where I was significant. And then I saw her, sat beside my name card at a linen-covered table. Dressed in the deepest green dress, her hair pinned high above her head. She was teasing the name card between her fingers nervously. I could feel my breathing speed up, but my legs slow down. Attempting to move closer, it felt like the room was dancing around me. And then she looked up.

ROMOLA

He was grinning at me, with the biggest smile I had ever seen on him. It was like watching someone see their life unfold exactly as they had dreamt, and I was a part of it. He looked incredible in his suit; the white shirt looked crisp against the darkness of his skin. His hair had grown out in the last few weeks, as the busy exam months had made it more difficult to visit a barber, but it looked amazing. As I watched him approach me he looked more playful and free.

"What has happened to you?" I joked. "You look like... you."

As I said it I realised just how much he had changed. It felt like there was no friction, like we could finally just be there. I knew that was partly because of me too, I no longer felt like I wasn't enough. There was no drastic change or life-altering surgery, just the simple understanding that I could affect my own life. That was enough for me to feel calm. I was nervous in a room of strangers, but okay in the knowledge that it was normal to feel that.

"How do you like the fro?" he laughed. "Should I keep it?"

"You most definitely should!"

I could feel my grin rising to meet his.

"You look incredible, Rome!" He said it with such conviction, it sent shivers straight through my stomach which danced in unison. I was watching his lips as he spoke, fighting the urge to lean forward to kiss him. After all it was still

Alexander Haywood, the hottest guy in school. To me he was the dorky kid who teased me, and sitting in front of me now there was nothing about him that felt out of reach.

"Would you like some wine?" Lex's mum asked us both, her words breaking the trance. "Only a little bit though, you're still kids."

"Thank you," I replied, tilting my glass towards the bottle of Pinot she was pouring for me.

"So, Romola, I hear you're not going to college next year?" she added, leaning in for a conversation. I pulled myself away from Lex, turning to face her.

"That's right. I'm doing an apprenticeship with a local newspaper."

"Wow, go you!" she replied with pride. "I always knew you were headed great places."

"Is that true?" Lex asked, steering the conversation back towards him.

I nodded.

"Yeah, I'm going to do it four days a week and then help my parents on the other days."

"That's incredible, Romola."

We chatted endlessly until the food arrived. As we spoke it was like there was nothing left to say, and yet there was everything. The night turned into a haze of lights and movement. Occasional conversations with other guests passed quickly and we were back talking about the past and future. I watched him as he spoke to family and he watched me as I spoke to others. There was no space between us, no matter how far away we were taken.

"Shall we dance?" he asked, peeling me away from his grandmother with whom I'd spent the past half an hour talking about baking with. He leant in and kissed her on the cheek.

"You're next." He smiled at her.

"I'll hold you to that," she joked.

"What are you doing this summer?" he asked as we danced closely. The music was insignificant, just a distant murmur against the heat of our bodies.

"I don't have plans." I smiled and for the first time those words felt like all my worries fell away. There was no pressure on the future, and I was excited for that.

"Good." He laughed. "So, we can finally end this game of cat and mouse?"

We were both laughing until we were kissing.

As we moved together surrounded by others, it felt like we were just two people with different identities. We were not stronger together, but stronger because we were ourselves together. The way I felt with Lex was like my world was falling inward and my legs would give away at any moment, but they were held up by me. In that moment we were together and it felt unparalleled. But there was no certainty in what lay ahead. With Lex I knew I would always have a friend, and where tomorrow would take us was unknown. The only thing I could be certain of was that I would always be living with myself.